A Shift in Darkness

A Lost Legacies Prequel Novella

Maddox Grey

GREYMALKIN

Cover Design by Seventhstar Art

eBook ISBN: 978-1-7375381-4-1
Paperback ISBN: 978-1-7375381-8-9

The Lost Legacies Series

A Shift in Darkness*

A Shift in Shadows

A Shift in Fate

A Shift in Fortune

A Shift in Ashes

A Shift in Wings

A Shift in Death

A Shift in Tides

*A Shift in Darkness is available for free download at
maddoxgreyauthor.com.

Quick Note From The Author

Hey there! I just wanted to chat real quick about what you can expect in this book. This is a fantasy novel that contains adult content and situations. If it was a movie, it would probably be rated "R" for violence, language, and sexual content. If you want to go into this book completely blind and prefer not to read content warnings, you can skip on ahead, my friend.

If there are certain topics that you need to avoid for the sake of your own mental health, or that you simply don't like, please take a look at the list below for some things you will find in this book.

- Emotionally abusive ex-lover with stalker tendencies
- Violent deaths of loved ones including parental death and death of a lover by abusive ex-lover
- Drinking alcohol as a coping mechanism
- Depression and panic attacks related to grief/trauma

Also... quick little note on language. I am a strange, strange person, and I've lived a bit of an odd life. I was born and raised in California, but was mostly raised by my Canadian grandmother and was then unofficially adopted by an Irish family in my late teens. You might be wondering why I'm mentioning this, and the reason is that I have a bit of a magpie approach when it comes to the English language.

Sometimes I like the American English spelling... sometimes I'm really attached to that extra "u" and go for the non-American version. Variety is the spice of life y'all.

Bless the soul of my copy-editor because she just sighs heavily at the start of each manuscript and deals with my eccentricities. So if you're an American and looking at a word and thinking it's not spelt right... it is most likely the non-American version of the word.

To the eastern glass lizard that bit me as a kid, and traumatized me for life. Thanks, buddy.

Chapter One

The exhilaration of finding my prey under the light of the moon never got old. I had been alive for centuries and had hunted all kinds of things in all kinds of realms. My brother and I had been born in the human realm, but our parents had been born in the feline shifter realm, Kanima. They'd told us bedtime stories of hunting across the vast open plains or stalking through the dense rainforests. My current hunt wasn't taking place in a location anything like what my parents had hunted in, but it was thrilling nonetheless.

The night was clear and the moon lit our way as we silently moved through empty backyards. It was well past midnight and all the humans were tucked away in their homes, built at the city's edge. I leapt over a tall brick fence and paused to take in my surroundings. Jinx landed on silent paws at my side.

"This is it," I said quietly and crept forward across the yard until I stood in front of a solid concrete wall. "The house we want is on the other side. Do you sense anything?"

I was good at sensing magic when it was in use, but I sometimes missed more subtle spells and wards unless I let my magic out to snoop around. Jinx stalked over to the pale concrete wall and sniffed it, then tentatively tapped it with a paw. He backed up a few steps, muscles bunching together, and then leapt upwards. He started the leap as an average sized black domestic house cat and ended it as a hundred-pound sleek feline perched on the top of the wall.

There is a ward directly on the other side. It's not designed to keep anyone out, just to alert its creator if anyone crosses it, his voice rumbled through my mind.

"Well, at least we know we found the house with the warlocks." I took a few steps back and then sprinted, jumping up at the last second. My fingers caught the top of the wall and I grunted as my body slammed into the concrete, then pulled myself up to crouch beside Jinx.

Smooth, Jinx said with a raspy laugh.

Shut it. I pushed the thought at him. *I didn't want to risk jumping too far and crossing the ward.* I scanned the area. The house was dark and no lights were on in the backyard which was mostly open. Like most of the yards we'd passed, this one consisted of several winding pathways that weaved through meticulously trimmed shrubs and elaborate rock structures. We would be easy to spot anywhere in the garden, not that it mattered. They'd know we were here as soon as we crossed the ward.

Plan? Jinx asked.

I pulled a throwing dagger from the sheath on my thigh and palmed it in my right hand. *Let's go say hello.* A wild grin spread across my face as I leapt down. A slight tingle ran across my skin as I crossed the ward. Jinx followed a second later. We didn't bother with stealth and stalked up the center of the garden towards the house. Halfway there, floodlights flipped on, and I heard movement from within the house. I stopped and drew in a breath, letting the scents linger above my tongue. Disappointment flickered through me. He wasn't here.

Damn it.

Two human men opened the sliding door of the house and walked into the yard. Their arrogant expressions gave them away as warlocks as much as their magic. The taller of the two looked at me and then at Jinx, a sneer spreading across his face. "I don't know who you are, but you and your fae companion picked the wrong house to intrude upon."

"We're just out for a neighborhood stroll," I said smoothly. "Hoping to meet up with a colleague of yours, actually. You wouldn't happen to know where Sebastian is now, would you?"

"Sebastian?" He glanced at his companion, who grimaced at the name, but shook his head. He focused on me once more, and then his eyes lit up in recognition. "You're that shifter he's so obsessed with. Heard what he did to that mermaid lover of yours. Nasty business." He grinned at me.

I went still at his words. The rage I carried with me always threatened to break the bonds I kept around myself. The chains I needed to make sure I stayed in control. Stayed alive. The warlock's grin grew wider, realizing he struck a nerve. Something deep within me rumbled.

Nemain, Jinx said in warning.

I drew in a deep breath. These warlocks would die tonight, but they'd answer my question first. I just needed to control myself for another minute then I'd make him regret his words. And that goddamn grin.

"I'm going to ask you one more time," I said coldly, gripping my dagger tighter. "Do you know where Sebastian is?"

"Even if I knew where he was, I wouldn't tell you," he said with a laugh. "I don't know what's got him all hot and bothered for you, which makes me curious to find out. And I've always been one to indulge my curiosity." He gave me a lecherous smile as he gestured at the other warlock. They quickly moved apart from each other, their magic rising. "I suggest you and the

3

grimalkin surrender yourselves to us peacefully, otherwise this is going to get ugly real fast. And don't bother screaming for help. That ward you crossed through blocks all sound from getting out. No one will hear your scream."

"Oh," I drawled. "It wasn't my screams I was worried about. But thanks for letting me know I don't have to worry about waking the neighbors."

I let the dagger fly as Jinx, and I unleashed ourselves on them. The warlock was true to his word about the ward, nobody heard their screams.

* * *

"Another dead end," I said tiredly. "No signs he was ever here." I flung the towel I'd been using to dry my hair on the floor and sunk onto the couch across from the mirror.

Jinx was sprawled out on the bed. He'd put his glamour back on for the trip back, but as soon as we made it back to our rented room he'd dropped the glamour again. Now his one-hundred-pound feline form was passed out, snoring slightly. I sighed. Moving him wasn't an option, Jinx was perpetually grumpy. Waking him up from a nap took him to a whole new level of grumpiness. He'd give me bad luck for a week.

"I told you I couldn't confirm any of the details about that lead, and that it was likely bogus," Pele responded from the large segmented mirror where her form took up the left panel.

She was looking at me with her unreadable neutral face she always used when overseeing meetings or negotiations between the various magical factions.

From the middle section of the mirror, Kaysea studied me, not bothering to mask her worried expression. It was a little jarring to see both of my friends side by side. With her deep red skin, fiery orange hair, and tall, lithe build, Pele was the opposite of Kaysea, who had pale white skin, dark green hair, and a short, soft and voluptuous build. I knew what both of them saw when they looked at me. To say I hadn't been taking care of myself the past few years was a bit of an understatement.

"It was worth checking out." I shrugged, wincing slightly at the pain from my shoulder injury.

Pele latched onto the movement before I could kill it. In the dimness of her office, her usually vertical pupils had dilated enough that her eyes appeared almost completely black, with only a slim sliver of turquoise around the outside.

"Has your shoulder still not healed?" she asked, leaning forward slightly in her chair as she studied me once more, looking for anything she had missed previously.

"It's fine," I said defensively.

"No, it's not." Kaysea frowned as she squinted at me. "You're clearly favoring your left shoulder. And that scar on your neck is still present."

I pulled my damp ash blonde hair over my shoulder to cover up the scar I'd gotten courtesy of a manticore. Their kind were devious and loved to scheme, I'd suspected that particular one had made a deal with Sebastian and I wanted to ask it some questions. It had taken offense to my line of questioning and buried its barbed tail in my neck. I hadn't so much walked away from the fight as limped, but the manticore hadn't walked away at all.

"Seriously, I'm fine. Everything will heal up in no time."

"Nemain, it should have healed weeks ago!" Kaysea crossed her arms and gave me her best no nonsense look. "Feline shapeshifters have some of the best healing abilities of any species. That neck wound should have healed within seconds, and that shoulder wound within minutes. And yet here you are, weeks later, still sporting a sore shoulder and a scar. That isn't *fine.*"

"She's right," Pele said calmly. "You've over taxed your magic and pushed yourself too far. Enough is enough, Nemain. You need to take a break."

"I need to find him! He's out there somewhere. I just need better leads, is all. Someone has to know something. It shouldn't be this damn hard to find one warlock!"

"You've been searching for him for decades, so clearly it is that damn hard," Pele snapped back. "I understand why you want to find him, I truly do, but even if you did, you're in no shape to fight him. You know Sebastian better than anyone. He's crafty and resourceful. You'll need to be at your best to take him on."

Rage shot through me at the mention of his name and the part of my magic I hid deep within me tried to surge out, but the chains I kept wrapped around it made sure it stayed contained. This was the other reason I looked and felt like hell.

On the surface, I was just a feline shapeshifter, but underneath, I was so much more than that. The magic I kept locked away would get me killed if anyone knew I had it. Even Pele didn't know the truth of what I was capable of. Although she had suspicions about some of it, I was sure. Kaysea knew everything. She was one of the few beings in existence that could claim such knowledge.

But even Kaysea didn't know how much I was struggling with keeping my magic locked down. It had been almost a year since I'd been somewhere safe enough to let it loose. Now it was raging inside me, fighting constantly to get free. It was draining and made me feel weary, both body and soul. Add onto that the number of fights I'd been in over the last six months and I was in rough shape. Still... they didn't understand. I couldn't stop now.

"I'll rest for a couple of weeks before following up on some of the other leads that came in," I lied. First thing tomorrow morning, I was planning on getting the hell out of this city. The Paris lead sounded promising.

"Liar," Pele said.

Kaysea opened her mouth, likely to argue with me more or announce she was coming to see me. "I'm tired. We'll talk about this more tomorrow." I cut Kaysea off and tapped the glyphs on the mirror. The surface of the mirror rippled and the images of my friends faded away.

Kaysea looked outraged at being cut off. Pele smiled. I knew that smile. My friend was plotting something and I wouldn't like it.

I glanced over at Jinx. He was still snoring lightly. I'd get dinner without him and just bring some up to the room for him to eat later. Pain shot through me as I lifted my shoulder to rotate it. Grimacing, I rotated it a few more times before gingerly lowering it once more. My friends were right to be concerned. I was pushing myself too hard. But I didn't have an alternative. Sebastian would never leave me alone. He would continue harassing me in my dreams and leaving bloody gifts for me on my birthday until I came back to him.

That would never happen. I had ended things with Sebastian a long time ago and moved on. At the time I thought he had accepted that. I found someone that I loved deeply and who loved me in return. Myrna. She was my everything. And she was dead.

I refused to live in a world where he still breathed and my love didn't. He was responsible for her death and he made sure she suffered in her last few minutes. I couldn't bring her back so I'd have to settle for cutting him apart piece by piece. I knew that this wouldn't make everything right again. She would still be gone. And I would still be lost. But it's all I'd had to keep me going.

Unfortunately, despite my skills at finding people and items,

I'd been on Sebastian's trail for decades and I had yet to kill him. Or even come close to it. Hell, I'd only managed to see him in person a handful of times, and that was only because he had carefully planned out those meetings and laid a trap for me.

But it didn't matter what my friends thought. It didn't matter that my body and magic were failing. It didn't matter that I woke every day with this bone-deep weariness and couldn't remember a time when I hadn't felt it. I wouldn't stop. Not until he was dead. What I would do after that or who I would even be, I didn't know. And I didn't care.

Chapter Two

After a quick shower, I headed downstairs to get some food. I could hear the chatter as soon as I opened the door to my room, breaking the quiet spell. It had been decades since I'd had a place I considered home. I never stayed in one place long enough to justify setting up something permanent.

Depending on where I was going, I would either sleep in the woods in my feline form or check into one of the many daemon run taverns scattered across the human realm. They varied based on location and who was running them, but they usually had rooms available for short- or long-term rent.

The ones I preferred to stay in were in towns that were also run by daemons because they usually had entire blocks dedicated to the magical folk. Humans who possessed magic could pass the wards to get into such areas, but they weren't really welcome and they knew that, so they stayed away. Despite living in the human realm my entire life, I cared little for humans. I was happy to avoid them when I could.

Unfortunately, that wasn't an option in Tokyo. The daemon tavern was in the Shibuya area of the city. Full of neon lights and popular restaurants and bars. The daemon youth loved it, and it was a popular destination for them when they came to the human realm. I couldn't wait to get out of this city and it's constant noise and weird organized chaos. Not that Paris would be that much better. As soon as I found and killed Sebastian, I'd hopefully never have a reason to set foot in another human city again.

"What can I get for you?" the daemon bartender asked when I slid into one of the last open seats at the bar.

I ordered several servings of sushi, enough to feed me and bring some back to Jinx. The bartender slid some sake in front of me and I gave him a flat look. He grinned, his white teeth standing out in sharp contrast to his dark red skin, and in one motion swiped away the sake and replaced it with a shot of whiskey. My lips quirked up into a brief smile before I snatched the whiskey up and slammed it back. He refilled my shot glass when I set it down and placed a beer next to it.

I swallowed the whiskey and then took a few sips of beer and planned out the next day. The daemons setup taverns like this for several reasons. Many of them liked to visit the human realm, and this gave them a place to stay while they were here. The taverns were also used as neutral meeting zones for daemons, fae, and other species. To facilitate all this, every tavern had a gateway that could be used to enter other realms or to travel to other daemon taverns within the human realm. Jinx and I could use the gateway here to travel to Paris and resume our hunt.

Halfway through my meal, the bartender slid a piece of paper in front of me. "Courtesy of Pele," he explained with a smirk, and then beat a strategic retreat.

I froze and slowly lowered the piece of salmon I'd been about to munch on before the bartender had made his ill-fated delivery. I knew that parting smile from Pele meant trouble, but

I'd thought I could escape this city before she ensnared me with whatever she was plotting. The blank paper stretched across the dark wood on a phantom breeze and stayed rolled out even as its edges curled inward slightly. With a fatalistic sigh, I reached out and tapped the paper, sending out the smallest amount of my magic with the contact.

Faint text appeared, and I waited a few seconds until it was readable.

Stop being a prat, Nemain. You need to take a break and since you won't listen to reason, I'm giving you two options. You can take this gig and get out of the human realm for a bit. It'll be easy for you and you'll make some money while you recuperate. Or you can refuse this gig and head off to Paris tomorrow morning. Yeah. I know about Paris. It's a bullshit lead and you won't find him there. You will, however, find me there. And I will personally throw your ass in a room and set a ward around it to prevent you from leaving until you've rested. Don't even think about running somewhere else.

I will find you.

Assuming you see reason and take the gig, I have a promising lead about Sebastian's whereabouts I'm willing to share with you. But only if you take the gig. Don't be stupid. Details on the gig are below.

Annoyance flickered through me. I knew Pele well enough to know she wasn't bluffing. If I didn't take this gig, she would track me down. I could avoid her for a while, but I couldn't hunt for Sebastian and avoid her. Not to mention, I relied on Pele to get more leads. I rubbed at my face, trying to wipe the exhaustion away, but that only made it worse.

"Fine," I muttered. "You win, Pele." I scanned through the next couple of paragraphs that detailed the gig. Pele had been arranging gigs for me for centuries and she was very thorough in vetting possible clients and information. Being a feline shapeshifter, I had a knack for finding lost things and people. I couldn't track by scent as well as lupines, but my senses were still far sharper than most species. Hunting was natural for me and I enjoyed it, even if it was just finding a lost artifact instead of a tasty meal. The magic that I kept hidden from others was particularly useful in realms with devourer activity which is why I'd slowly built up a reputation as someone who could pull off jobs in those realms. Pele made sure that no one asked questions about why I was able to do such a thing. It was a setup that worked out well for us, but it also meant that Pele had suspicions about my magic. She was one of my oldest friends so we'd danced around it this whole time, she didn't ask pointed questions and I never flaunted my magic in front of her. As a high-ranking daemon, it was one thing for her to suspect and another thing to know with absolute certainty. I didn't want to put my friend in a situation where she had to choose between her loyalty to me and to her people.

Pele was right, this would be an easy gig. There wasn't any way I could rush it either. If I agreed to do it, it would commit me for roughly a month. That was more than enough time for my body and magic to recuperate, especially if I found some time on the trip to sneak off and let all of my magic loose for a bit. The only problem would be Jinx.

The gig was a straightforward one, but the clients had specified a no fae rule. Being a grimalkin, Jinx was technically fae. I could ask them about it when I spoke with them tomorrow. They likely had a problem specifically with the sidhe, so maybe they would be okay with a grimalkin.

I speared the piece of salmon with my chopsticks and

plopped it in my mouth, enjoying the flavor as I chewed. While I hated most things about this city, I loved the food. Assuming I took this gig, which I almost certainly would, I'd be eating dried fruits and meats for the duration of the journey. Or whatever else we could pack and carry. It was unlikely there was anything in that realm that was edible. I grimaced at the thought. The gig may not be as challenging as the ones I often did, but it definitely wouldn't be a pleasant trip.

The bartender glanced in my direction and I waved him down. "Cool if I take the rest of this upstairs?" I gestured towards the board with the remaining sashimi. He nodded, and I picked the board up, weaving my way through the growing crowd and headed back up the stairs. Jinx stirred slightly when I opened the door to our room.

Is that dinner I smell?

"Yes, I can get you more if you want," I told him and placed the wooden board on the floor.

Jinx half fell, half slid off the bed and walked over to where I'd placed the food. Between one step and the next, he put his glamour back on and a small black domestic cat crouched down to delicately eat the sushi.

I'm going to miss this, he said after he'd finished all the salmon pieces and moved on to the tuna.

"About that," I started, and Jinx paused his eating, golden eyes wholly focused on me. "Pele arranged a gig for me. It's escorting a small group to some sacred places in their home realm. It's a super easy gig and it'll give me a chance to rest. But one of the stipulations is that no fae are allowed. I can ask if they'll make an exception for you, but if they don't, you could stay here and wait for me. Eat all the sushi you want."

Who is the gig for, and where is it? He sat back and continued to glare at me. I'd really been hoping the promise of being able to eat sushi for the next month would be enough to distract him. It'd been a long shot, but it'd been worth a try.

"The Kalari." Jinx twitched his whiskers mildly in distaste. I huffed in amusement.

It didn't matter the species, all fae were snobby assholes when it came to magic. I'd met some Kalari in passing a long time ago, shortly after they came to the human realm. They were empaths.

While some of them had been quite strong they had no other magic and no interest in playing politics. Which meant neither the daemons or fae had any interest in them. I stretched out across the bed and propped myself up on one elbow. It was better to stake a claim on my half of the bed before Jinx jumped back on it and tried to hog it all again.

"A few families are joining together to make the trek, and they need an escort. Given the state of their realm, it's not like there is anything there to harm them, but they don't want to take any chances."

Pele vetted them? Jinx asked, and then went back to eating. Some of the tension eased out of me. "Yes. Her and Kaysea are worried about me. This is Pele's way of forcing me to take a break."

All right. Ask them if I can come along. If they won't allow it, then I'll wait for you here. Where are you meeting them?

"Daemon bar in Cairo. I'll head there in the morning and ask about you. If they say yes, I'll send for you. Otherwise, I'll confirm with you when I'm leaving and then come back here after I drop them off when the gig is complete. It should take a month, maybe a little less if we get lucky and find what they need early on in the trip."

Jinx finished eating and raised one paw, licking it carefully before doing the same to the other. I flopped down on the bed, stretching my arms above me as I yawned. A moment later, I felt the dip in the bed as Jinx jumped up and then curled up beside me.

It will be good for you to get away for a while, Jinx said carefully.

I squeezed my eyes shut as a heaviness weighed on me. It was easy to push off Pele's and Kaysea's concern, but Jinx was different. He'd been my companion since I was born and we'd been through a lot together. He wasn't the lovey dovey type. He would never say he was worried about me, but I'd heard it in the way he'd carefully chosen those words. He hadn't put up much of a fight either about me going off on a gig on my own.

"Yeah," I said quietly. "I'll do this, recover a bit, and then we'll go back on the hunt."

Chapter Three

"Nemain?" a daemon with light purple eyes asked as I walked through the gateway the following morning.

I blinked at the sudden brightness of the room. The daemon tavern in Tokyo had been dimly lit, as if they wanted to give those who entered a reprieve from the flashy lights of the city.

The Cairo tavern was its stark opposite. A large skylight let in the morning rays of the sun and the walls were painted a light tan, with darker swirls that reminded me of sand dunes. Spices drifted on the air from whatever they were cooking up in the kitchen and my stomach grumbled even though I'd eaten breakfast before leaving. Maybe I'd have time for second breakfast.

"That's right," I said, after getting my bearings and stepping away from the gateway.

"Pele said to expect you. I am Sura. Right this way, please." She opened the door and held it open for me.

I followed her into the rest of the tavern that was mostly empty. Daemons preferred the night and most would be sleeping now. A few tables were occupied, but not by daemons or fae. Instead, sphinxes, dryads, and some hooded figures sat

16

around the bar, quietly conversing. No sign of my clients. They must already be in a meeting room upstairs.

Sura led me through the tavern, nodding in greeting at the green-eyed daemon behind the bar. The decor and style of daemon taverns varied, but their layout was usually the same. I wasn't surprised when Sura led me to some stairs towards the back of the bar that lead up to the second floor. This floor was usually for meeting rooms while the third-floor rooms were set up for lodging. The daemons likely had another building or two in the city where more long-term lodgings were available.

We walked down a wide hallway until Sura slowed and opened a door. "They're waiting for you inside and can provide you with the full details of the job and answer any of your questions. I shall oversee the meeting as a witness."

I nodded my thanks and stepped inside the large square room. A round table sat at its center, easily able to seat twenty individuals. More seating was arranged along the sides of the room. The Kalari occupied all but one of the seats at the table and most of the seats along the walls.

I scanned the group quickly. I'd only met a handful of Kalari in the past, but there was nothing remarkable about them. They had always looked similar to humans and this group was no different. Most of those gathered had varying shades of brown skin and dark hair, but there were a couple with pale skin and light blond hair. The Kalari had originally settled in this area of the human realm, but over the generations they had spread out more. They seemed to be more comfortable living amongst the humans than with other magical species.

Whatever they'd been discussing died down as they all turned to stare at me. I'd twisted the ring I wore around my left index finger prior to coming to this meeting to dispel the glamour I usually wore. As far as I knew, the Kalari couldn't see through glamours so I could have kept it up. But we'd be leaving the human realm for this job so there was no reason for me to keep it on, and despite the insistence of my friends that there was no way for me to feel the glamour when it was activated...I did. It made my skin feel tingly and annoyed me. So I usually switched it off whenever I wasn't traveling around in the human realm. This meant that the Kalari saw the true me. If they were startled by my golden-brown skin with lighter rosettes and my cat-like bright green eyes they didn't let it show. I supposed compared to the daemons running around the bar I wasn't exactly the oddest creature they'd encountered here.

I approached the table and stood by the empty chair closest to the door. "Greetings, I'm Nemain. It's my understanding you're looking for help in searching for some sacred sites in your old realm?"

An older Kalari rose from her seat and gestured for me to take a seat. Based on the wrinkles that lined her face and the way she held herself, I was guessing she was in her seventies or eighties. The Kalari had a slightly longer lifespan than humans from what I remembered, typically living well past a hundred. I slid into the chair as she spoke.

"Yes, thank you for coming, Nemain. Pele spoke very highly of you. I am Sekeela." She eased herself back down into her chair and I caught the worried look of a younger Kalari next to her. Likely her granddaughter based on their similar appearance and the difference in their ages. Both of them had light brown skin and upturned eyes, framed by curly dark brown hair. Sekeela's eyes were a deep honey brown that, despite her age, still shone brightly.

"Can you tell me more about what you need? I know the basics about your home realm, but not much, and I've never been there."

The Kalari sitting closest to me rose and walked over to a

side table, where he poured a cup of coffee. He sat the steaming mug down in front of me along with some cream and sugar.

"Thank you," I murmured as I wrapped my hands around my salvation. I could give up a lot of things, but coffee would never be one of them.

"Since falling to the devourers centuries ago, our home realm, Kalarin, has been lost to us. The last person in my family who had been to the realm was my great grandmother." Sadness crept across her features as she spoke and part of me softened at her words.

I'd never known the realm of my parents, it had also fallen to devourers and I'd seen that same lost expression on their face when they talked about it.

"Every few decades the daemons would allow some of us to go back to check on the realm. Most of the time, those who went never came back. But almost a hundred years ago we discovered the volcanoes in our realm were erupting on a massive level. It was too dangerous for us to explore at that time, but we did our best to check on it every decade since. From what we can tell, the entire realm was impacted by the volcanic activity. Nothing survived, including the devourers." Sekeela smiled grimly. "Unfortunately, even without the devourers, we still can't return to Kalarin."

"Because of the volcanic activity?" I asked, trying to remember what I'd heard about the realm. I'd never sought information about it because unless one were a Kalari, the fate of Kalarin didn't matter to you.

Devourers was a catch-all term we used for species that had evolved to eat the magic of others. Nobody knew where they had come from, but the human realm was full of survivors who had lost their home realm to them. The only reason the human realm hadn't been overrun by devourers was because the fae and daemons protected it, along with their own realms and a few others. But that type of protection was expensive, and realms like Kalarin hadn't been able to afford it.

"Yes," Sekeela said. "The volcanoes stopped erupting decades ago, but up until recently, the air was far too toxic for us to venture into the realm. There are no signs of life, plant or animal. Ashes cover everything, at least from the areas that we've been able to get gateways opened in." Her voice cracked, and she coughed. The young Kalari, who I thought was her granddaughter, retrieved some tea for her before picking up where Sekeela had left off.

"We believe it's safe enough now for us to go back, for a limited amount of time," the young Kalari explained. "It's not safe enough for us to move back permanently, and truth be told, I'm not sure many of us would choose that even if it was an option. The human realm is the only one I know. Most of us have as much human blood in us as Kalari at this point. But we believe it's safe enough for us to return for a short time."

"To what purpose?" I frowned and took another sip of coffee.

"What do you know about us?" she asked. "About the Kalari, I mean."

I leaned back in my chair. "Not a lot," I admitted. "It's general knowledge that you are empaths, but since the Kalari have mostly integrated with the humans, you've largely forgotten about by the rest of the magical community."

"We *were* empaths. We aren't anymore."

"You lost the ability?" I cocked my head to the side. There were other species that reproduced with humans. Sometimes their magic changed through the generations, but the humans actually had quite a bit of magic. They just didn't know how to use it. Most of them, anyway. I'd never heard of any species losing their magic altogether because of the human blood that had entered their lineage. I knew of shifters that were mostly human at this point, but could still shift.

Sekeela put her tea down and patted the young Kalari woman on the arm. "Our empathic abilities came from two places," she explained. "From our blood and from the underground water springs that were common throughout our realm. Without that water, our abilities remain dormant."

"That's why some of the Kalari kept trying to go back, even when the realm was crawling with devourers?" I guessed. "They were trying to access the springs?"

Sekeela nodded. "We don't know how many of the springs are still accessible. Many of them were likely destroyed or covered by debris from the volcanic eruptions. But we have to try. Despite us losing our abilities most of us have kept in touch over the generations. If we can find those springs and work with the daemons to build a gateway close to them, we can regain what we lost."

"Do you have any idea where to start looking?"

"Yes. Our ancestors created maps of many of the spring locations. We've reviewed them and will start in the area that is most likely to prove successful."

"All right," I said slowly. "Did your ancestors say anything about what type of devourers had invaded your home realm?"

"Not in any great detail," Sekeela said regretfully. "There were quite a few different kinds. Most seemed lupine in nature. There was a reference to some swallowing Kalari whole from beneath the surface, but we don't think this is true. Earthquakes were common in our realm and sometimes large sinkholes would form out of nowhere. Most of us agree that this is what happened and that some of those fleeing the devourers were unlucky enough to experience such a fate."

"Fun." I grimaced. "I accept the job and can leave today if that works for you. I have one request."

"We will hear your request and honor it if we can."

"My companion often comes with me on these jobs. He didn't come this morning because one of the stipulations of this job was no fae and he is a grimalkin. Would you allow him to come with us?"

The atmosphere in the room changed immediately, and I knew what the answer would be even before Sekeela spoke. "I'm afraid that won't be possible," she said, her expression stony. "Kalarin was a beautiful realm and my people were well known for their empathic abilities. It may not be the most powerful of magics, but it can be quite useful for healing psychological trauma. There were a lot of gateways to the fae realms throughout Kalarin because the fae, the sidhe especially, liked to visit our realm. When the devourers invaded and my people were forced to flee, the fae promised to keep the gateways open and protect us as we fled. It was a lie. The fae only held the gateways open long enough for any visiting fae to get out, and then they closed them. Leaving my people to die. We will never forgive them for that."

"I understand," I said, and I wasn't lying. The realm my parents had been from suffered a similar fate. The fae only looked out for themselves. It was a lesson most of us had learned the hard way. "I will let him know. When will you be ready to leave?"

The tension in the room eased at my acceptance of their decision. Sekeela gave me a grateful smile. "We can leave within the hour."

* * *

I slung my pack over my shoulder as I waited for the Kalari to join me in Sura's office where the gateway was located. Jinx hadn't been pleased about the news that he wouldn't be joining me, but we knew this was a likely outcome.

Sura was able to provide me with food rations that would last the duration of the trip. The younger Kalari, who I guessed were mostly in their early twenties, would have to carry both their rations and the rations of the older Kalari that couldn't carry as much. I was a little worried about Sekeela and some of the older individuals. They had selected a region to explore that had once been an expansive plain with some hills, but we had no idea how much of that had changed since the volcano had exploded.

There was also the concern about the air quality. Even though my healing ability was a bit sluggish these days, it should be able to keep up with healing my lungs as I breathed in the toxic air. Sura had provided some enchanted cloth masks for the group to wear that would help, along with some healing potions. But none of the Kalari in the group had any magic, and even if they did, the Kalari had never had any physical healing abilities.

I'd have to keep an eye on the group and be ready to get them out of there if the masks and healing potions weren't enough. I wasn't sure exactly how I would do that. The Kalari didn't know about my abilities, as far as they were concerned I was just a feline shapeshifter. If I had to, I could open up a gateway at any time and get us out of there, but I really didn't want to reveal that ability to them.

A glimmer of color caught my attention, and I spotted a bin full of bright gems sitting on a shelf. I walked over and looked at the roughly cut gems and thought of an idea. I looked over my shoulder at Sura, who was studying me curiously. "Mind if I grab one of these gems? I usually bring something with me as a good luck charm," I lied. "I can pay you whatever it's worth."

She shrugged. "They're just common gems we use for amulets and other trinkets. There's nothing special about them and they're not worth anything in their current state. Feel free to take one."

"Thanks." I rifled through the gems until I found an impressive looking red one. I held it up in the sunlight and it refracted the light beautifully. Perfect. I reached into my bag and pulled out a bit of wire and wound it around the gem in a simple, but secure pattern and then tucked it away in a leather pouch attached to my belt. Hopefully, I wouldn't need it, but it would do in a pinch.

Sekeela and the other Kalari joined us in the office a few minutes later and waited by the gateway. There were twenty-seven of them in total, mostly family units. I spotted the young Kalari who was indeed Sekeela's granddaughter in the back of the group chatting with some of the other Kalari who were her age. Sekeela cleared her throat and everyone in the group fell silent.

Sura bowed her head in thanks and then stepped forward to stand in front of the gate. "I will open this gateway in the designated place in Kalarin at sunrise each day until you return. Even though we do not believe there are any devourers remaining in the realm, it is not safe for me to leave open at all times." I nodded in acceptance. This was standard protocol whenever I went to realms that were unknown or had previous devourer activity. "When you locate an active spring and decide that's where you'd like a gateway to be established, send a pulse of magic into this gem and bury it in the earth. Upon your safe return, I will put in a request to activate the gateway." I plucked the dark blue gem from Sura's palm and dropped it into my leather pouch with my other gem. I understood what Sura wasn't saying. If we didn't return within a reasonable amount of time, the daemons would assume we died somewhere in the realm and they wouldn't bother building a gateway there. Or come to check on us.

"Thank you, Sura," I said. "Everyone ready to go?"

"We are," Sekeela replied. Sura smiled and turned to the wooden arch of the gateway. She delicately traced some glyphs into a wide section of the polished wood and the air within the arch rippled. My magic itched under my skin at the feeling of a gateway opening and I pushed it down, keeping my expression blank and calm. A few seconds later, the gateway fully opened, revealing a desolate landscape in front of us.

I wrapped the cloth mask around my face, tying it snuggly behind my head, and stepped through. Thick layers of ash cushioned my steps and bits of it rose into the air with each step. I took a dozen steps away from the gateway and looked around, grimacing as I waved everyone through.

Sekeela was last and paused by my side. "I had tried to prepare myself for this, but..." She trailed off and I understood what she meant. It was morning, but the sun was completely blocked out, leaving us in a dimly lit realm surrounded by nothing but ashes. There was no life here. The sky and ground were both a desolate grey and there were no other hints of color that I could see. At least in this area the land was completely flat as if a giant had used their hand to sweep everything away. I'd been to realms that had experienced mass extinctions and there were at least large skeletons or the remains of trees left behind. Some proof that life had once been there. But here there was nothing but ash and emptiness. I imagined what Jinx would say if he saw this. Probably something along the lines of, *lovely place.* The ashes would have driven him insane. He hated anything that clung to his fur.

"Good luck," Sura called from the gateway. The contrast between the lovely daemon with her vibrant purple eyes and deep red skin standing in her sunlight office, surrounded by the dead realm, seemed cruel. I waved my goodbye, and the gateway closed. The Kalari gathered around me expectantly. I was impressed they weren't letting the bleakness of the environment dim their hopes.

"Let's head north," I told them. "We'll travel for a bit and get an idea of what the terrain is like and then likely camp in the late afternoon while we plot out tomorrow's path." I started us out at a steady pace. With each mile in the barren landscape, I hoped Sura's wish of good luck would be granted. We would definitely need it.

Chapter Four

"We can rest here for the night," I announced several hours later. We'd made steady progress all afternoon towards our first potential spring location. I'd mostly left the Kalari to talk amongst themselves as I scouted the area around us, always making sure to keep them in my sights in case they veered off course. Or something dangerous came their way. But this realm appeared to be truly and completely dead.

The Kalari gathered around me. "It's up to you if you want to set up your tents tonight. There's nothing around to burn so we'll have to make do without a fire. But the temperature has remained consistent all day, I don't think it will get that cold at night." Sekeela nodded in thanks and the group started getting settled for the night.

Bedrolls were laid out before they all sat down and shared their food with each other. I did a quick perimeter check before returning to set up my own bedroll. I would have preferred to sleep in my feline form, but the cloth I had tied around my face wouldn't work in that form. I had taken it off for a little while when we'd first arrived just to see how bad it was and quickly put it back on. It felt like breathing in smoke and gravel. Even with the mask on the air tasted foul. So I wouldn't be shifting unless I had a damn good reason to.

A young Kalari girl offered me some dried fruit, but I waved her off, instead chewing on a piece of jerky while I contemplated our trip. Sekeela and the older Kalari had done well today and I was significantly less worried about them being able to keep up with our long travel days. That might change if the terrain got rougher, but we might get lucky and find a spring in this area which as far as I could tell was flat in every direction.

Gradually, the chatter among the Kalari died off as they fell asleep. I listened to their steady, deep breathing under the starless sky as I dozed on and off. If I was lucky I'd have a dreamless sleep, but I knew the chances of that were slim. Sleeping meant dreaming, and dreaming meant nightmares. Eventually sleep pulled me under and soon I was running through a dark forest, my heart pounding in my chest as fear raced through me. Slowly I was able to pull myself out of the dream just enough to realize something wasn't right. As if feeling my awareness, the rainforest faded away and I found myself seated at a table in a brightly lit room with no doors.

My heart hammered in my chest as I took in my change of scenery. There were only two dreamwalkers in my life and my brother would never have done something like this. He knew that I hated dreamwalking and only approached me this way if he had no other options, and even then, he was much politer about it.

"Sebastian." I spat out the name as he came into view and took a seat across from me. His blond hair was tied back neatly at the nape of his neck and his light blue eyes were alight with amusement.

"Hello, my love. Your mind is distant tonight, I take it you're off on an adventure in a different realm?" I clenched my jaw at his casual words and the corners of his lips tilted up. "Still angry at me I see. That's a shame, I only want you to be happy."

"Bullshit!" I hissed as my nails dug into the table. "I don't know what the fuck you want with me, but you don't give a shit about my happiness. If you did, you would have left me the hell alone!"

"You would be happier with me." He casually shrugged one shoulder. "That mermaid was only a temporary distraction. I grew tired of waiting for you to see that so I thought I'd hurry things along."

I lunged across the table, but my fingers closed around nothing but air. Sebastian smirked at me from where he now stood, several feet behind the table. As a dreamwalker, Sebastian had complete control over this dream. I couldn't hurt him here and I knew that. But that had never stopped me from trying.

"Why don't we have this chat in the human realm?" I asked, not even bothering to make my voice sound pleasant. "I've been looking for you, but you haven't been taking my calls."

He laughed. "You left quite the mess in Tokyo. And London before that. Something tells me you don't want to chat so much as try and rip my head from my body. I think meeting like this is a more productive use of our time." He gestured around the room before studying my face. "You look tired Nemain, are you not sleeping well?"

"Maybe if you stayed the hell out of my dreams I would sleep better."

"We both know you wouldn't."

"Fuck you."

"I was hoping your anger would fade over the decades, but I should have known better." Sebastian shook his head regretfully. "You still haven't gotten over the death of your parents and it's been centuries. Your ability to hold onto rage and grief is as impressive as it is tedious."

"What do you want, Sebastian?" I couldn't hurt him in this dream and staying here was just making me angry. My control over my magic was already strained and this wouldn't help. If I'd been in a better state of mind I might have been able to get him to slip up and give me some clues as to where he was, but I was exhausted. Besides I was good at a lot of things, but being clever in conversation was never one of them, definitely not against Sebastian.

He paused, a thoughtful expression on his face. "It's been a while since we spoke, I wanted to check in on you and see how you were doing. Your birthday is coming up and I haven't decided what to do for it yet. I think it should be special this year."

I went still at his words. Ever since Myrna's death, Sebastian had left a gift for me every year on my birthday. Usually a bloody heart. Sometimes I knew who it was from, sometimes I didn't. Occasionally, he'd drape jewelry or other gifts over it. If I wasn't in the human realm for my birthday he would leave it somewhere in the human realm where I would find it. Or he'd leave it at the home of someone I knew, as a casual reminder that he knew me well. And he knew who I loved.

It was one of the many reasons I spent most of my time in the human realm. I wanted to find him. I needed to find him. But even if I wanted to walk away from this and leave it all behind me, Sebastian wouldn't. He'd find those I cared about one way or another and use them to draw me out. So I stayed in the human realm as much as I could, only taking the occasional job outside of it.

"Yes, I think this is the year for us to step things up a bit," he murmured, his eyes darkening.

Something about his tone made a shiver run down my spine. In a physical fight, Sebastian was no match for me. But he was devious and patient. I needed to figure out whatever he was plotting so I could stay out of his trap. My mind raced, trying to think of things to ask him that would clue me in on what he was thinking.

His features smoothed out and he gave me a charming smile. "Do be careful on whatever job you're on. You and I aren't done yet."

He snapped his fingers and I jolted awake on my bedroll. All of the Kalari still slept soundly around me. I drew in several ragged breaths before forcing myself to calm down. Sebastian wasn't in this realm and I wouldn't be back in the human realm for several more weeks. There was nothing for me to do, but let my body and magic heal. Something told me I would need to be at my best for my birthday this year. Sebastian was plotting something new.

Chapter Five

W e trekked across the ash-covered landscape for two weeks, checking all the possible spring locations that had been fairly close to where the daemons had originally opened the gateway. None of the locations marked on the map had worked out. I had suspected as much when we reached the first location and we found nothing there that looked even close to what had been described. Even though this region wasn't directly in the path of the volcanic activity, it had clearly been altered drastically since the Kalari had left the realm.

A long time ago, this region had been valleys nestled in-between rolling hills. The valleys still existed, although they were now covered in thick layers of ashes instead of grassy plains, but the hills were no longer hills. They were mountains. We had checked what we could in the flat lands, the next location would require us to travel over the mountain.

Sebastian hadn't visited me in my dreams again. I'd been trying and failing not to obsess over what he could possibly be plotting for my birthday this year. Whatever it was, there was nothing I could do about it currently. These past couple weeks had been good for me, I was already feeling considerably stronger than I did at the start of our trip. Whatever Sebastian was planning, at least I would physically be in better shape. I still needed to find a way to release my magic for a bit, just to take the pressure off. But an opportunity hadn't presented itself yet.

We'd started the hike up the mountain this morning, but soon we'd need to make camp before it got too steep to do so. Sekeela never once complained or asked to slow down the pace. I still kept it fairly slow and took breaks fairly often under the pretense of making sure we were heading in the right direction in this harsh landscape.

The Kalari were an interesting group. Mostly, they acted human, which made sense given how much they had integrated with the humans over the generations. But there was still something wholly unique about them. Even though they claimed not to have a lick of magic left in their blood, they still reminded me of the empaths I'd been around.

Over the weeks, I found myself talking to Sekeela and many of the others about all kinds of things. It was odd to converse about mundane topics with people who were practically strangers to me. But I found I didn't mind it.

"I think that area over there will do well for camp." I pointed to where some large boulders had fallen on top of each other to create a nice, sheltered area.

The group followed me over to the boulders and I walked in between the two of them to see how much space we had to work with. Seeing there was plenty of room for everyone, I let them all lay out their bedrolls, and then I stretched mine out at the top of the entrance.

Sekeela laid out her bedroll next to mine and carefully sat down. Aki was chatting with the group of younger Kalari while setting up her own bedroll, but she had snuck glances at her grandmother to make sure she was all right.

"She's very attentive." I observed.

A wide smile spread across Sekeela's lips. "She's a mother hen."

I snorted, a small smile playing across my lips.

"She's always been that way," Sekeela continued. "When she was barely two years old, she'd make sure that all the other kids had their snacks before she did. She had a cat with long fur that she would very carefully brush every night. It had to be the most patient cat in the world to put up with her constant fussing."

Jinx would never let me brush him. He claimed I did it wrong and messed up his fur. I had once tried to tie a bow around his neck when I was a kid, and he had acted like I tried to strangle him. I'd sobbed, and he'd eventually relented and let me do it.

Just the one time, he had said. After fixing the bow around his neck, I'd shifted into my feline form and made my brother tie a matching bow around my neck. Jinx and I had pranced around the house all day while my parents just watched us with amused expressions.

The smile on my lips died.

"Something the matter?" Sekeela asked, sensing the change in my mood.

I shook my head and dug out my dried meat and water from my bag. "It's nothing. Just thinking of my parents." I snuck a piece of meat under my mask and chewed slowly.

"I take it they are no longer with us?" she asked softly.

I shook my head slowly, and she looked at me with kind eyes. I looked away quickly and took a drink of water.

"Aki's father was my son. He and her mother both died in a car accident when she was six years old. She was devastated by their loss, as any child would be."

My throat tightened, and I wrapped up my remaining food, tucking it back into my back.

"I know talking about such things can be hard," Sekeela said gently. "And I don't mean to pry. It just seems like you're in pain, and sometimes talking to someone other than friends and family can be easier. But I won't push." She held her hands up like I was a terrified animal and went about getting her own food.

"Thank you," I said, my voice rough. "I'm going to check on the others." I stood up quickly and walked around the small space.

The Kalari had adjusted to the harsh situation much better than I thought. They were clearly tired, but their overall spirits were good. They were excited to be back in their home realm and on this journey, so close to reclaiming what they had lost.

Aki was talking to two other young girls, both with their backs to me. One of them leaned forward and said something the others apparently found hilarious because they all started giggling. The one who told the joke glanced over her shoulder at me and smiled.

My heart seized as I met her light green eyes. She didn't look that similar to Myrna. The eyes were almost the same shade, but Myrna's skin was a creamy white and her hair was green, this girl had light brown skin and dark hair. But there was a kindness in this girl's face tinged with mischievousness that was so much like Myrna.

Thinking about my parents had knocked me off guard and now I was spiraling out of control. The magic that I kept hidden deep within me pushed at its bindings and I felt them weaken, soon it would break free. I'd waited too long to let it out and now I was out of time.

I needed to get out of here.

"I'm going to do a quick perimeter check," I said to no one in particular. "Everyone, stay here and I'll be back soon."

I forced myself to stride calmly out from the rocky outcropping and away from everyone else. Only when I was sure I was out of everyone's sight did I break out into a run. Where could I go? I needed somewhere to contain my magic. If there was a lake, I would have leapt in it, but there was no water to be seen. Just ash covered rocks and earth.

My foot tripped over a rock that jutted out of the ground and I almost fell flat on my face. I recovered at the last possible second and then looked back. Where the rock connected with the earth, a crack had formed. I slowly walked along it as it widened until eventually I was looking at a large opening in the earth.

A sinkhole.

I could just barely make out a tunnel leading down. A cave must have formed at some point. I glanced around, but in the growing darkness I couldn't see anything else that would work. Another surge of my magic had me scrambling down into the inky darkness.

* * *

I was only dimly aware of my surroundings as I plunged deeper into the cave. With every step, I felt my magic breaking free. It took all my effort to place one foot in front of the other and continue my descent. My fingers dragged along the cold earth on each side until it widened enough that I could no longer reach. Still, I kept going. Within seconds, it was dark enough that the little light from the moon no longer reached and my exceptional night vision failed, leaving me completely blind.

I kept going, embracing the darkness.

Unable to see anything in front of me, my mind kept playing images over and over again. My parents burning. Myrna's broken body. I had failed everyone I'd loved.

Finally, the ground leveled out, causing me to briefly stumble. My breathing was ragged, and I took a few trembling steps forward before falling to my knees. The final chains I kept wrapped around my magic fell away. Crystal blue flames erupted from me, bathing the cavern in light as it licked the walls.

I let out a deep sigh of relief as the flames surged around me. My ability to open gateways into any realm might get me killed. The fae and daemons certainly wouldn't like that I could easily get through their defenses. But they might find a use for me. But not if they learned about this part of my magic. This *would* get me killed.

The devourers were the boogeyman of our world. Many species made up the devourers, but the one thing they all had in common was they could absorb the magic of other beings. Hence the name. Most of them were also immune to magical attacks, making them a deadly opponent. Of all the ones that had been encountered, none had been capable of communicating. They had a keen predatory intelligence, but nothing more.

I was a feline shapeshifter. My parents were feline shapeshifters, as was my brother. All of their magic was normal feline shapeshifter magic. I had the magic of feline shapeshifters running through my veins, but I also had devourer magic.

Such a thing shouldn't have been possible. My ability to open gateways into other realms was strange enough, but perhaps feline shapeshifters had been capable of such things and we just didn't know. There weren't many of us left and much of our history had been lost. But there was no explanation for the part of my magic that devoured. It even felt different from the rest of my magic. It hungered and constantly wanted to be free of the cage I kept it in.

My breathing steadied as the flames continued to swirl around me. It would have been better if there was some magic here for the flames to devourer so that it could satiate that part of me. But this would have to do for now.

I shivered slightly; the air in the cave was cold and the sweat drying on my skin didn't help. I felt my magic shift slightly until it coated me like a second layer of clothing and I instantly felt warmer even as frost began to form on the cave walls. As if the devourer magic that manifested as blue flames wasn't weird enough, it left frost in its wake. If there had been anything in this cave to burn, I would have left behind ashes and frost.

"We can't stay much longer," I murmured to it, even though I knew my magic wasn't sentient. Not truly. But sometimes I wondered if it was something close to it.

Gradually, the flames receded until they danced along my arms. I raised my right hand as I rose, flames moving up my arm until they flickered in my palm, lighting the way forward.

I trudged back up the tunnel, adjusting and tightening the cloth mask around my face. The air hadn't been as bad in the cave, so I hadn't bothered to fix it when it'd come loose.

Cool night air brushed against my skin when I reached the surface, I paused and looked up at the night sky. It was odd to not be able to see any stars. Similar to how the sunlight was spread out amongst the overcast skies during the day, the moonlight was also diffused across the sky with only the barest light of the moon itself visible. I usually loved the night, as I was nocturnal by nature. But this world felt haunted during the day and it felt even more so at night underneath the eerie sky.

The sooner we found a water source here, the better. I never wanted to return to this realm again. Shaking off the unsettling feeling, I headed back to the camp at a brisk jog. My mind felt more settled and my magic once again slumbered deep within me. It wouldn't last long, but it would have to do for now.

When I returned to the human realm, Jinx and I would go on the hunt again. Once Sebastian was dead and rotting, I'd let myself fully rest and heal. Maybe then my soul would piece itself back together.

Chapter Six

"Do you think we'll find anything today?" Aki asked as we slowly made our way to the top of the mountain. None of the Kalari had said anything when I returned last night, but I felt their concerned looks on me all morning. I'd expected Sekeela to walk with me and try to get me to talk about my parents. But to my surprise, after she'd cheerfully greeted me good morning, she'd been spending time with each member of the group. Aki joined my side not long after we set out, but she'd been content to be silent until now.

"I don't know," I answered honestly. "We should be coming up on the spring that was marked on that map soon. But the terrain in this area has changed considerably since it was created. According to the map, we should be in a valley right now, but instead we're still hiking up this mountain." I stomped my feet a little, causing ashes to float up with each step. "Plus, the ashes are heavy on this side of the mountain, everything is likely covered by feet of it."

Aki frowned. "This was one of the few places in the realm the daemons could reliably open a gateway to. The other two places were a short distance from the volcano and we figured our chances wouldn't be high there of finding water. If we don't find water in this region, we'll have to barter with the daemons to start opening gateways in random areas of the realm where we won't be able to plan out our trips according to our old maps."

I opened my mouth to tell her that while we might have an old map of this area; it was proving to not be all that useful, but I stopped myself. She was already feeling discouraged. There was no need to add to it. "Things might look more promising once we get over the top and start heading down the other side. It's possible that the ash fall won't be as heavy beyond this ridge."

"That's a good point." A bright, wide smile spread across Aki's face. "I'll tell the others."

She spun around in excitement and tripped on some uneven ground.

I grabbed the back of her jacket to keep her from face planting. "Careful."

She sheepishly grinned at me and steadied herself. I released her jacket, and she made her way to her friends, keeping her steps slow and careful.

An hour later, I looked at the landscape stretched before us from the summit. There was indeed a valley on this side, but I couldn't tell yet if the ash fall was less. I grimaced as I brushed at the sleeves of my jacket and gray dust flew off. The ashes got everywhere.

At this point, it felt like it was ingrained in my skin and I'd have to soak for weeks when I got back to get it out. The masks the daemons had made for us were still working well. I'd noticed the air tasting a little less foul. I wasn't sure if that was because of our altitude or because I'd just gotten used to it.

"What do you think?" Sekeela asked.

I'd told the Kalari that we would take a break here and most of them were resting and eating a light lunch. Sekeela and another older handsome Kalari man had come to stand next to me as I scanned our surroundings. I was fairly certain the man's name was Bahir. He'd been splitting his time between a young couple and their two children and Sekeela. It seemed likely he was related to the family, probably the grandfather of the young children. I hadn't been able to figure out his relationship to Sekeela exactly. He'd been sneaking glances at her all morning, which she was either ignoring or didn't notice.

"I don't think the spring marked on the map in this location still exists," I said evenly. "Even if it does, the landscape has changed so drastically we'd have to spend a lot of time trying to find it. But once we make it down this mountain, the terrain seems to mostly match up with the map. This means there is a decent chance the other spring is still there. We won't know until we go a bit further how much ash has spread across this area."

"How long do you think it will take to reach it?" The man asked. He had a deep, calming voice. It reminded me of my father's voice. My throat tightened, and I pushed the thought away. I needed to get myself together and focus on the task at hand.

"Three or four days." I toed the ground in front of us. "Getting down this mountain will likely take us two days. The footing is slippery and there are some jagged rocks jutting out of the earth on this side. If someone slips and falls, it could result in a serious injury. We'll need to go slow."

"Very well." The man nodded at me and held out his arm to Sekeela. "I have some extra dried fruit I can share with you. I brought extra mangoes that you like." Sekeela smiled at him, her eyes alight with delight. "Thank you, Bahir. That is very kind." She took his arm, and they walked away.

I watched them for a few seconds. He was clearly in love with her, and there was definitely love in that smile she gave him. An ache tore through me and I looked away from them. Taking this job might have allowed my body and magic to recover, but it sure wasn't helping my mind. It had been centuries since my parents had been murdered. Decades since Myrna had died. But I still couldn't let them go.

My life had revolved around avenging my parents. I'd briefly known peace with Myrna before Sebastian ripped her away from me, my life once again tumbled down into darkness. I'd thrown myself into the hunt for Sebastian, but without that to distract me, I kept turning to dark thoughts that were as desolate as this realm.

Not much longer, I thought. We'd find the spring and then I'd open up a gateway to get us out of here. I'd figure out a way to explain it. The Kalari would get what they needed and I could go back on the hunt and put my mind to rest.

The good news about the downward trek was the ash was indeed considerably lighter on this side of the mountain. There were large stretches where I could actually see the earth underneath. The downside was that it piled up in some places and disguised the slippery shale like rock that littered the slope. I'd almost fallen a few times, and only my feline flexibility had saved me from falling flat on my face. They weren't exactly graceful saves, though, and I was glad that Jinx hadn't been able to come with me because if he'd seen me waving my arms frantically as I regained my balance, he would have cackled manically the whole way down.

The Kalari weren't so fortunate. We'd already had several nasty falls. No one had broken anything yet, but we'd had to pause twice to apply some makeshift bandages to stop the bleeding. We'd made it almost halfway yesterday before stopping to make camp. Our pace this morning had been slow and if we didn't pick it up, it would be dark before we reached the bottom. As I made my way carefully around some jagged rocks, I noticed some upturned earth. Odd.

I made my way over and crouched down to examine it. Bright red earth was mixed in with the ash as if it had been stirred up in this spot. A thin trail led back to some slabs of shale that had stacked on top of each other, and I peered underneath, searching for where the trail led.

"Did you find something?" Aki asked from behind me.

"I'm not sure," I replied and stood up, brushing off my hands. "Let's keep going. There's no way we can make camp on this incline and it's going to get even more treacherous as it gets dark."

"I'll try to help the others move a little faster."

I watched her go and check in with the others and looked back at the trail that led under the shale. It went too far back for me to be certain, I'd have to crawl on my stomach to get far enough under the shale to confirm, but it looked like there was a burrow back there.

Unease rippled through me. We had seen no signs of life and I didn't know how anything could have survived the devourers and the volcanic activity. If something did survive, my money was on the devourers. But even they had to eat. They needed a supply of magic to sustain themselves. Not to mention this realm had been through hell with all the volcanic eruptions. Nothing could have survived on the surface. It didn't seem possible for anything to have survived all this time. But that trail had looked relatively fresh, days old at best.

Once we made it down the mountain, I'd ask Sekeela and the others to tell me again what they knew of the devourers that had invaded their realm. For now, I needed them to concentrate on getting down this mountain safely and quickly. No need to add to their worries just yet. I gave one last lingering glance at the trail and then headed back towards the rest of the group.

The Kalari had spread out as they carefully chose their footing. Sekeela was with Bahir and his family. Aki was assisting one of the older Kalari, and most of the younger ones had paired off to help their elders. I surveyed the group and decided to check on those in the back. I was halfway there when a scream caused me to whirl around, barely keeping my balance on the slippery slope. I looked just in time to see Bahir fall forward and land badly on his shoulder before tumbling further down the mountain and slamming into a large piece of shale. Even from where I was standing, I heard bones crack.

Bahir didn't rise or make a sound.

"Don't move!" I shouted at Sekeela and the others in their little group as one of them leapt forward to help and almost fell herself. "Stay with the others! I'll get him!" I moved forward quickly, trusting my instincts to keep me from falling.

The ground slid out from under my feet, but I kept going, reaching Bahir in moments. I felt for a pulse, relief running through me as I felt a steady throbbing.

"He's alive!" I called over my shoulder.

The rest of the Kalari were getting close, but they were being careful about their descent. I quickly ran my fingers over Bahir's body. His shoulder was definitely dislocated, and I thought maybe his collarbone might be broken.

Ash and blood covered his dark brown skin making it hard to tell where the wounds were. Most of the cuts and scrapes looked superficial. I pulled up his shirt and carefully checked his ribs.

Once again, I thought some of them might be broken, but I wasn't sure. I didn't have much experience treating wounds since my own magic would heal most injuries I was dealt. I knew some basics only because it was easier for broken arms and legs to heal if you got the bones in the right position. But I had no idea what to do about possibly broken ribs and a collarbone. One thing was for sure. He wouldn't be walking the rest of the way down this mountain.

"Fuck," I growled in frustration.

Sekeela reached my side and quickly knelt to check on Bahir. The rest of the group kept their distance to let her work. "Broken collarbone. Dislocated shoulder. Ribs are bruised, but I don't think they're broken. His left knee is swelling pretty badly. He must have struck it on the way down." Her voice was detached and clinical as she continued to examine him. Only the tightening of her eyes gave away her concern and fear. "We need to finish getting down this mountain so I can clean and patch him up the best I can."

I pursed my lips as I studied him and then looked at how much we had left to travel. Probably another two hours of slowly picking our way down. Ugh. This was going to suck so much.

"Can you stabilize his injuries the best you can?" I asked and adjusted my pack and weapons. "I can carry him the rest of the way."

Sekeela glanced up at me in surprise. "You can?"

I smiled tiredly at her. "Yeah, it won't be fun, but I'll manage."

Bahir and I were roughly the same height, just shy of six feet. My usual thick muscular frame was running a little lean these days, but I still wasn't a lightweight by any means. Even so, Bahir likely outweighed me by sixty pounds. Being a feline shapeshifter, I was stronger than humans, but not by a lot. Speed was more our thing than strength. Still, I could manage this. It would be easier if I could strap him to my back or carry him over my shoulder, but that likely wouldn't be good for his injuries.

Sekeela and the others used extra clothing to wrap Bahir up so that he wouldn't cause further damage to himself. He didn't stir while they carefully worked on securing the bandages. I could already see the bruise forming on the side of his head beneath the ash and blood, but at least it wasn't bleeding too bad.

"All right," Sekeela said. "That's the best we can do."

I knelt down and carefully picked Bahir up, trying hard not to jostle him as I rose. He was awkward to hold this way, and it put me off balance. I leaned back on my heels slightly. "Nobody else fall, okay? One injured Kalari is the most I can handle." Steadying myself, I concentrated on putting one foot in front of the other as I made my way down the mountain. The Kalari followed on silent footsteps.

Chapter Seven

"Well, he will not be walking anytime soon," Sekeela said.

I nodded. She'd confirmed what I already suspected. The rest of the Kalari were getting settled for the night on a large, flat boulder.

While everyone had been climbing up onto the rock, I'd noticed these piles of shale that had stacked on top of each other, creating a small cave. There was only room for a few people inside it, but we decided it was best to set up Bahir here. He still hadn't woken, but we'd managed to get some of the healing potion into him. The cuts and scrapes had already scabbed over, and if he had a concussion, it should help with that as well. It also meant we wouldn't have to worry about any infections. But the healing potion had limits, and broken bones were one of them. He'd heal faster than he would otherwise, but it would still be several days before he could walk again and that was if we were lucky.

"We have a couple of options in front of us," I told Sekeela. "We can wait here as a group for Bahir to heal enough to walk and then continue on. The path ahead of us looks relatively flat, so it won't be as hard of a hike. Depending on how fast we can travel, it will take us between one to two days to reach the area marked on the map."

"We're so close," Sekeela murmured as she absently fixed the blanket she'd wrapped around Bahir. She glanced up at me, a steady intellect gleaming in her eyes. "I take it you have concerns about us waiting?"

"The enchanted masks are working, but not enough. I can already tell that your breathing is more ragged today than it was yesterday. We only have so much healing potion, definitely not enough to go around and heal everyone's lungs."

"We thought that might be a problem, but I hoped we'd have more time. What do you propose?"

"Split the group up. I don't like it, but I think it's the best option if you want to continue searching for a spring." I paused, choosing my words carefully. "Ideally, it will be those that can travel swiftly because we'll need to get to the spring and travel back to join the rest of the group and then make our way back to the gateway." I left out that depending on how everyone was doing and my own impatience, I would likely open a gateway when the group was back together. I'd already come up with a cover story for how I was able to do such a thing. But I didn't want to tell Sekeela and the rest of the Kalari that part of the plan now, because that would give them more time to ask questions and poke holes in my explanation.

"I suppose this journey is really for the young ones anyway," Sekeela said as she turned to study her granddaughter.

"What do you mean?" My brows rose in confusion.

She turned back to look at me, smiling softly. "I never planned on drinking any of the water here. None of us from the older generation are."

"But you're so close," I said. "You know all about your

heritage and the magic that comes with it. Why would you turn away from that now?"

"We all have our reasons and I can't speak for the rest. But for me, I've lived my whole life without empathic magic. It hasn't stopped me from being able to understand what others are feeling and help them through it. I might have to work harder for it, but I'm proud of that. I only have so many years left in me. If I were to drink the water from this realm and gain empathic magic, I don't know what that would do to who I am. I'd have to relearn so much." She laughed quietly. "I might be a stubborn old fool, but I've earned that right."

"Will you watch over him while I speak with the others?" Sekeela asked.

I nodded absently, and she rose after tucking in the blanket around Bahir one last time. I watched her walk over to where most of the other Kalari were gathered.

The smaller groups moved in to join the rest when Sekeela gestured them over. I didn't know what to make of Sekeela's and some of the older Kalari's decision to not drink the water from this realm. It had never occurred to me that some would turn down the chance of having magic.

Deep within me, my own magic shifted slightly before settling down, as if it was letting me know it was still there. I loved my shifter magic. Being in my feline form was as natural to me as my human one. My ability to open gateways into any realm would get me into a lot of trouble if others found out, but I still enjoyed it. It allowed me to travel to realms that most wouldn't dare or had never even heard of.

But the other part of my magic. The part that rippled beneath my skin like a beast wanting to be set free... I didn't know what I would do if I was given the choice of having that magic or not. My life would be so much simpler if I didn't have it. And truth be told, it had only caused me pain. But the thought of not having it felt odd, like a part of me would be missing.

I shook my head, trying to clear the thoughts. There was no reason to dwell on it because I had never been given a choice in accepting my magic or not. I had been born with it and had been dealing with it my whole life.

Bahir stirred slightly, and I knelt down next to him, getting ready to keep him down if he awoke with a start. His dark eyelashes fluttered, and he slowly opened his eyes. "Easy," I told him. "Don't try to sit up." He didn't try to rise, but he started to raise his arm and sucked in a breath as he grimaced in pain.

"How bad?" he asked, his voice hoarse.

"Broken collarbone, dislocated shoulder, banged up ribs, and some serious damage to your knee." I grabbed a bottle of water from my bag and helped him take a few sips. "But your face still looks pretty for Sekeela, don't worry."

A deep chuckle rumbled out of him, and he instantly winced. "I thought I was being subtle about it."

"No, you didn't."

"True enough." Bahir's eyes lit up in amusement. "I was subtle for a few years and it got me nowhere, so I thought I'd try a new approach."

I huffed a laugh. "Try not to move too much. The healing potion is still working, and it's going to make you tired. Get some more sleep if you can."

Bahir gave me a tired smile, sleep already pulling at him, and closed his eyes. I leaned back and sat in a more comfortable position to wait for Sekeela to return so we could plan out tomorrow, and to ask her exactly what she could remember of the tales from this realm. I hadn't forgotten about that trail I spotted on the mountain.

Something was still alive in this realm, and I was about to leave an injured Kalari behind with a group of Kalari with no magic or fighting skills. I'd have to think of a way to protect them so they didn't end up as something's dinner.

* * *

A slim Kalari woman with dark hair and eyes came over a short while later and knelt down on the other side of Bahir. He stirred slightly, but didn't wake. She was the woman who was part of the small group that Bahir usually walked with. I had assumed that either she or the man were the child of Bahir, because the teenagers traveling with them were definitely his grandchildren. Now that she was in front of me, the resemblance was undeniable. "You're his daughter?" I asked.

She nodded. "I am Yareera. Thank you for watching over him. The rest of the group is ready to speak with you now. I will stay with my father."

"If he wakes, make sure he doesn't move too much." I tucked my food and water back into my bag and stood up to join the others. The rest of the Kalari were gathered in a half circle on top of the boulder, Sekeela and Aki towards the front. Aki didn't look happy and Sekeela seemed to be working too hard to keep a pleasant expression on her face. Oh boy.

"What has the group decided?" I asked.

"Those who are capable of traveling quickly will leave with you in the morning. The rest of us will stay here and watch over Bahir while we wait for you to return. If you reach the area where the spring was marked and you're unable to find it, then you'll return to the rest of the group and we'll make our journey back to the gateway. We'll simply try again in the future."

"All right, and it's been decided who is going and who is staying?"

"Yes," Sekeela replied. "Aki will be going with you and she

will make sure everyone is ready in the morning." Aki's expression hardened further, but she didn't argue.

"Okay, that plan works for me."

Without Sekeela and some of the older Kalari, we might have even been able to find the spring tomorrow before nightfall. Then we could rejoin the group the next day and I could get everyone back to the human realm. And resume my hunt for Sebastian.

Pele and Kaysea wouldn't be very happy with my trip being cut a little short, but I was already feeling significantly better. I'd need to plan for a day or two when I got back, anyway. That was enough time for my body and magic to finish recuperating.

The anticipation of being back in the human realm soon almost made me skip my question about the mysterious trail I'd seen earlier in the day, but common sense won out. Most of the gigs I took through Pele were to find lost artifacts, and it was usually just me and Jinx on those adventures. But I did escort jobs like this one often enough, and I had built up a solid reputation over the years. Pele vouched for me, which meant a lot. If there was something still alive in this realm, I needed to know.

"What can you tell me about the devourers that invaded this realm?" I asked. "You mentioned before that some of them were lupine in nature, but others came from the underground?"

Sekeela frowned. "Most of us don't believe those stories. This realm has always had lots of earthquakes and it was common for large cracks in the ground to open up. We think the stories just got embellished over the years."

I rubbed my jaw and studied the stone beneath our feet. It was a good ways off the ground. I was able to jump to the top, but the Kalari had to climb up its steep sides. It likely went even further into the earth. Nothing was tunneling through this. We'd have to move Bahir up here, which would be difficult, but if there was something still alive in this realm and it moved around through a tunnel system, I couldn't leave him on the ground. I'd stay with him tonight and then move him in the morning. That would give the healing potion a few more hours to work, at least.

"Why do you ask?" Sekeela asked, concern flickering in her eyes as she looked towards the shelter where Bahir rested.

"When we were making our way down the mountain earlier, I noticed a trail," I said. "I'm not completely sure, but it looked like it led to a tunnel underneath some shale. It was too dark for me to get a good look at it." The Kalari shifted and many of them looked off into the night. This realm had been depressing and unsettling to travel through, but it hadn't felt dangerous to them because we had assumed that we were the only things living here.

"Are you sure it was a trail?" Aki asked. "Maybe it was just a weird pattern formed from the way the wind was blowing the ash?"

"It was definitely a trail, and it was horizontal against the slope, so it wasn't from a rock or debris falling. I don't have any explanations. It doesn't seem possible for anything to have survived in this realm. I've only seen that one trail and we've seen no other signs of life. But if you decide you don't want to take the chance of splitting up the group and would like to return to the human realm, I would understand."

Aki and Sekeela discussed it with the others. I paid enough attention to keep track of the conversation, but in my head, I was already thinking about different options if they wanted to continue onward or if they wanted to return to the human realm.

If they decided to return, it meant I'd be able to get back to tracking Sebastian that much sooner. I suspected they would decide to stay, though. They'd come this far and turning back now, especially after Bahir had been injured, would feel like admitting defeat. It might be the smarter thing to do, but I knew that Aki and the rest of the younger generation were getting excited about the real possibility of getting their magic back. While Sekeela was content to continue living her life without it, this would be life changing for them and it was unlikely they'd want to turn back when they were so close to feeling magic coursing through their blood.

"We're in agreement then," Aki said. "We'll keep going, but we need to figure out what to do to protect those who stay behind." She focused on me. "Any suggestions?"

"To be clear," I said evenly. "There is an inherent risk with this plan. Whatever left that trail behind could be completely harmless. It could be a common predator, or it could be a devourer. If anything was going to survive all of this, my money would be on a devourer, but I'm not sure how it would have survived this long." I tapped my foot on the rock. "Nothing is tunneling through this, so you don't have to worry about anything coming up from the ground. I'll stay with Bahir tonight, but we'll move him up here in the morning. Then you'll need to set up a rotation for guard duty, try to leave the rock as little as possible."

"Should we move Bahir up here tonight?" Sekeela asked.

"I'd rather give him a few more hours to heal. It's going to be difficult to not jostle him as we get him up here. I can protect him from anything that comes." I pulled the longer of the swords that I kept strapped to my back loose. The Kalari all went still as they looked at the blade. "For those who are staying behind, do any of you have any experience with weapons?"

I let out a sigh as I saw nothing but blank stares. Then a tall Kalari man stood up from the back of the group. "I've been practicing martial arts my whole life and I've done some practice with kendo," he said. I raised my eyebrow in question, and he smiled. "Japanese fighting with a sword."

"Good enough," I said as he wound his way to the front of the group. "I don't have a spare scabbard so you'll just have to be careful," I told him, holding the sword out to him, hilt first. He gingerly took it out of my hands and studied it. He clearly wasn't a fighter, but at least he wasn't holding the sword like it would bite him. "Everyone should get some rest tonight. I'll keep an eye on Bahir and the rest of the group."

The Kalari offered the sword back to me and I shook my head as I pulled my other sword out slightly from its scabbard before sliding it back. "I'm good. Keep it with you at all times and practice handling it, so if on the off chance you have to use it you don't stab yourself."

"Don't you need to get some sleep, too?" Aki asked.

"I've gotten plenty of rest already. I can go days without sleep and be fine. I'll see all of you in a few hours." I turned and leapt off the rock, going back to Bahir. I told Yareera to return to the group and watched her go, making sure she made it safely back. Then I sat down at the opening of the shelter where I could keep an eye on Bahir and the group and waited for dawn.

Chapter Eight

I waited patiently a short distance ahead for Aki and the others who would be coming with me. Getting Bahir up onto the boulder with the others hadn't taken too long. After considering the options, I'd found the lowest part of the rock and jumped up with him. The landing jostled him a bit, but we didn't do any further major damage. The last I saw of him, he was doing his best to look pathetic while Sekeela doted on him. I caught his eye as I was leaving, and he gave me a wink when he thought Sekeela was turned away. From my vantage point, I'd been able to see both the wink and Sekeela rolling her eyes.

I'd expected a larger group to be coming with me, but it was only Aki and seven others. The Kalari were trying to remain calm, but I suspected they were more shaken up about the mysterious trail than they wanted to admit. Some of those staying behind did want to get their magic back, but they didn't want to leave the most vulnerable of their group alone.

The Kalari were confident the daemons would construct a gateway closer to the spring, so future groups of Kalari would have the opportunity to access the spring. I hadn't told them yet that if there truly was devourer activity in this realm, the daemons wouldn't allow the construction of any gateways here.

Since I hadn't seen any solid evidence of devourers, I'd kept this information to myself. They'd already had enough bad breaks on this trip, I didn't see any reason to give them more potential bad news. Sekeela likely already knew this anyway since she had been the one to negotiate with the daemons for this trip.

I pursed my lips as I watched Aki leap down from the rock. I was usually much better at keeping myself distant from clients and everyone in general, but I'd started to like the Kalari over the past several weeks. They didn't want their magic back to gain power or improve their status in the magical community. Instead they wanted to use their gifts to help people. I'd scoffed at their claim at first, centuries of bitterness making me unable to believe they didn't simply want power.

But they were honest and genuine. They truly did want to help people. It still seemed like such a foreign concept.

"Ready," Aki said when she reached me. She quickly went over everyone's names again, somehow knowing that I hadn't memorized the names of everyone in the group.

I recognized two of them as Bahir's grandchildren. All of these Kalari were young like Aki, probably in their late teens or early twenties. I wasn't always the best at telling how old humans were. To them I probably looked like I was only a few years older even though I was actually centuries older. Most shapeshifter species lived for thousands of years, we were similar to the fae and daemons in that regard. Eventually our magic would start to fade and then we would start aging again until our magic left us completely, then death would finally claim us. Dying of old age was rare in the magical realms. We were a violent lot.

"We're going to travel fast," I told the group. "If we're lucky, we'll be able to find the spring before nightfall, then we can travel back tomorrow. But say something if you need to take a break, especially if you start to have trouble breathing. Understood?"

Everyone nodded, anticipation lighting up their eyes. Even Aki, who was clearly concerned about leaving her grandmother behind, was eagerly shifting her weight from foot to foot. They were likely all excited about the thought of having magic by the end of the day. I'd have to monitor their breathing as we went.

I didn't trust the young, idealistic fools to say something if they started to struggle, and I didn't want to deal with yet another injury or serious health issue. I turned and set out at a brisk walk. It would have been easy for me to travel for miles at a steady jog, but I knew the Kalari wouldn't be able to keep up that pace.

I scanned the ground as we went, but I didn't see any other trails. There was very little ash in this area and the soil was a rusty red color. I'd been to dozens of realms, but I'd never seen anything like this. Large obsidian crystals jutted out of the ground. Most of them had to be well over twenty feet tall. The further we traveled, the denser they got, until it was like we were traveling in a forest of jagged crystals. Most had a shiny black surface, but there was a slight variation to some of them. Deep blood red. Dark amber. Twilight purple.

"This would be spectacular in true sunlight," Aki said as she sped up to walk by my side. I grunted in agreement. She smiled as if my terse response amused her. "I'm guessing you've been to other realms? Like the fae and daemon ones?"

"Yes."

"Have you ever seen anything like this?"

"Nothing exactly like this," I admitted. "There is a cave deep underground in one of the fae realms that has large crystals like this. But they're not dark, they're more like glass, but slightly opaque. It's not frequently visited because the only way to reach it is through a tunnel that is underwater. I only know of it because a friend of mine is merfolk, and she was able to bring me."

"That sounds incredible. I'd love to be able to see other realms."

"Not content in the human realm like most of your kind?"

"I don't mind the human realm. I'm not sure if I'd ever live somewhere else." Aki studied a large crystal in front of us that had split into multiple pieces. Even with the overcast sky, the dark blue surface sparkled in the light. "I just want to experience more."

I shrugged. "Even if you don't get any magic from this excursion, you could still visit the daemon realms. It's not common for beings with no magic to travel outside the human realm, but the daemons wouldn't make that big of a deal of it. I wouldn't suggest going to the fae realms." I thought about it. "Actually, even if you get your magic back, I wouldn't suggest going to the fae realms. Not unless you have a travel companion who knows their way around. The fae aren't friendly to outsiders."

"I've heard that." Aki laughed softly. "Do you still travel around with your merfolk friend?"

"Uhhh...no. Not recently. I've had other things to occupy my time."

"Is she the one you lost? Or connected to whoever it was?" My head snapped towards her, but she kept her gaze straight ahead. Her expression was even and calm. When I didn't answer, she explained. "I see the way you look at Sekeela and Bahir. You're as amused by their ridiculous dancing around each other as the rest of us, but something dark always flickers through your eyes after a while. Watching them, in their obvious love for each other, hurts you."

"Here, I thought it was your grandmother I had to watch out for," I said tightly. "But it's you who sees far more than you should and asks questions you don't have a right to ask."

"I'm sorry," Aki said quietly. "I meant no harm by it, truly." She fell silent, but continued walking by my side. Her steady presence reminding me of Kaysea.

"She wasn't lost," I finally said. "She was taken from me." I couldn't bring myself to say killed. Murdered.

"What was she like?"

I swallowed, heat building behind my eyes as we kept walking. "She was the opposite of me in many ways. Kind and softhearted. She laughed freely and often. The mermaid that I traveled around the realms with was actually her sister. That's how we met originally."

"Was it love at first sight?"

"It was," I said softly. "For both of us. Kaysea, my friend and her sister, was happy for us. But their older brother, Connor, never approved. He didn't like the idea of his baby sister living outside the sea. Of everyone in the family, her magic was the weakest. It never bothered me, and most of the time, it didn't bother her. She loved to paint, and I always teased her that her artistic skills were better than magic, anyway."

The blue flowers that were tattooed on my back and arms itched, but I refused to rub at them. The one in the center of my back, the one that my love had painted, burned the most. Some of the Kalari had asked about the tattoos in our conversations, but I'd made it very clear that I didn't want to discuss them so they'd dropped the topic. My magic remained oddly still within me even as my emotions churned.

"Most of our culture has been lost over the generations," Aki said. "Or it's blended in with the local human culture of wherever we live. But there are some things that we've managed to keep. One of them is honoring the dead. Once a year, all Kalari gather in one meeting place, always by the sea. On the night of a new moon, when the stars are at their brightest, we kneel in the waves and whisper the names of our loved ones so they will know that we still remember. That we still love them."

I couldn't bring myself to speak as my throat went dry and my heart pounded in my chest. I hadn't whispered her name into the waves of the sea. I had screamed it until my throat was raw and my voice was nothing but a memory.

"Will you tell me her name? I will speak it on your behalf."

The tightness in my throat eased enough for me to whisper one word. "Myrna."

Chapter Nine

We made it to the area marked on the map by late afternoon. Aki had steered our conversation towards lighter topics after asking me about Myrna. At first, I'd kept most of my answers short, but gradually she drew me into the conversation more. It didn't take long for the rest of the Kalari to join in our conversation, asking me about the different realms I had been to and what the fae were like. Most of them had interacted with daemons at some point, because daemons had towns and safe houses scattered throughout the human realm. But the fae rarely came to the human realm, and when they did, it was usually with a purpose allowing them to get in and out quickly.

I learned more about the Kalari, too, especially the younger generation. This group, in particular, had always been interested in keeping the culture of their ancestors alive. While many of them were like Aki, and didn't think they would ever actually live anywhere else besides the human realm, they wanted their magic back. It had been the younger generation that had pushed for this expedition to see if they could regain what they had lost.

When we reached the edge of where an outline had been drawn on the map, I paused for a break. I knelt and spread the map out on the ground with all of them crouching around me. "This is where the spring was originally located." I pointed toward a spot on the map that was probably a mile away from us. "We know the volcanic and tectonic activity has changed the land a lot in this realm. We crossed a damn mountain that hadn't been there previously. The exact information on this spring was vague, but I think it was located in a cave system underground. We'll head to the exact location on the map and start our search out from there."

"Should we split up when we get there?" Aki asked. "To cover more ground?"

I shook my head. "I'm not taking any chances. We stay together as a group and search for what we can today. If we don't find anything, we'll make camp when it gets dark and then search for a few more hours in the morning before going back for the others. We can leave the marker somewhere here for the daemons to construct a new gateway so that when the second group comes back, they can at least begin their search again here."

Aki and the others nodded, their expressions optimistic and determined as if they could will the spring into existence. I gathered up the map and took a long drink of water before continuing onward. The large crystal formations continued in this area, but were spread out more. They helped improve the landscape, but the lack of plant and animal life was wearing on me.

It hadn't rained while we'd been here, but I'd seen some signs of rainfall, so it did happen. I just didn't know how often. If the Kalari wanted to kick-start plant life in this realm again, they might need to import some seeds and accept that the native flora was gone forever. The daemons would know if there were any suitable plants from other realms that might survive here.

"What's that over there?" a Kalari with wavy blond hair and dark brown eyes asked. I looked at where he was pointing. Several dark red crystals had pushed up out of the earth and into each other. Beneath them, there was a large opening into the ground.

"Let's go check it out," I said, walking over and crouching by the cave mouth. "It's not that deep. I can see the floor. I'll go first and then call out for you to follow."

"Okay," Aki said, practically vibrating with anticipation.

I hopped the six feet into the cave entrance and then headed farther in. At first, I had to crouch, but the path leading further into the cave had a slight decline, soon I was able to stand upright. The air was cool and damp, but not stale.

Scattered across the ceiling were gaps to the surface. Some of them were big enough that I could see the large crystals above. They let in more than enough light for me to see clearly, and the Kalari should be able to navigate easily enough. The path continued leading straight back, and I followed it until it reached a large open cavern. One side of the ceiling was completely open to the sky above. Beneath it, water bubbled up from the earth, forming a stream that sparkled in the dim lighting before winding its way through a narrow passage further in the cave.

Even from where I stood, I could feel the slight trickle of magic from the spring. I let out a sigh of relief and then called out over my shoulder, "Come on in, Aki! You're gonna want to see this!" The sound of the Kalari jumping into the cave and hurrying down the cave followed. Aki reached me first and gasped when she saw the spring. The others gathered around and all of them stared at the water in amazement.

"We found it," Aki breathed.

"Now what?" One of the other Kalari asked.

"That's up to all of you," I told them. "We'll plant the

marker near the mouth of the cave so the daemons can create a gateway here. All of you have to decide if you want to drink the water now, or take some with you and drink it later. I don't know how long the magic of the water will last away from the spring."

Aki frowned. "We don't either. All the information we have about the springs and the rituals of our ancestors involved drinking the water directly from the spring. They never mention what happens if you bottle it up and carry it away." Slowly, like she was in a dream, Aki walked over to the stream and crouched down. She reached out with trembling fingers and let the water run through them. "I don't want to wait." She looked up at the others and they nodded at her. All of them walked over to the stream and crouched down.

"Let us become what we were meant to be," Aki said. The young Kalari scooped up water with two hands and drank it down. Seconds passed. Then minutes.

"Do you feel that?" The blond boy who had pointed out the cave earlier asked.

Aki stretched her arms out in front of her and stared at her hands. "It feels like something is waking up inside of me." She turned her attention to me and her eyes widened. "I can feel you!"

"That's not creepy at all," I said dryly.

Aki laughed, tears of happiness running down her cheeks. "I'm going to look around outside a little bit. All of you stay in here." A chorus of agreements answered me and I beat a hasty retreat. The last thing I wanted was a bunch of new empaths to take turns reading my emotions.

They could practice on each other for now. One of the first things empaths learned was how to not automatically read the emotions of others. The world full of dark thoughts and feelings. The Kalari youth would learn that quickly, but I could give them at least a few moments without my darkness.

* * *

The Kalari stayed in the cave while I explored the nearby area. I stayed close so that the cave was always within eyesight and that I would hear if they shouted for me. Some upturned dirt caught my attention by one of the crystal formations, and I knelt down to examine it. The earth had clearly been disturbed, but it wasn't a trail, instead it was more like a circle.

"Weird." I brushed the dirt aside, but there was nothing underneath. The dirt outside the circle was undisturbed. I spun on my heels and scanned the surrounding area, but didn't see anything else out of place. The sooner we got out of this realm, the better. I looked up at the rapidly darkening overcast sky. The floor of the cave was solid rock, so we'd camp in there for the night and then head back first thing in the morning.

I made my way back to the cave and found Kalari kids rapidly talking to each other in excitement about what they were feeling. I cleared my throat to make sure I had their attention since they hadn't even noticed me enter the cave again. Their chatting quieted down and several of them gave me sheepish looks. "We'll sleep in the cave tonight and then leave at first light to join up with the others. I know all of you are really excited about your magic, but I would advise that you don't read me. First, it's rude. Most empaths can't help but get surface emotions from other beings, but if you try to dig any deeper, it can be felt. Best case, you'll offend someone, worst case they'll kill you for invading their privacy."

The excited expressions slid off their faces as they took in my words and thought about the serious repercussions of their magic. Good. Empathic magic came with a lot of baggage. Some argued that it was even more invasive than mind reading because mind readers could be tricked, or sometimes beings lied to themselves enough that it was hard to shuffle through their thoughts. But it was hard to fake emotions on anything other than a surface level.

"Second," I continued. "You'll find the emotions of beings such as myself... aren't exactly made up of sunshine and rainbows. Reading darker emotions can haunt you, especially since you don't have the context to go with them. Understood?" I met the gaze of each Kalari, and they each gave me a solemn nod in return. "Good. There is still some light left. I'm going to place the marker outside this cave. Aki, if you want to come with me, I'll show you where it will be."

Aki quickly stood up and followed me out of the cave. I walked a short distance from the cave opening and then pulled the marker out of my pocket. The dark blue gem hummed with magic and felt warm against my skin. "I'm going to activate the marker," I told Aki. "It will construct the physical structure of the gateway, but it won't actually be functional until the daemons push magic into it."

"Do you need me to do anything?"

"No." I pushed a small amount of my magic into the gem and it started to glow slightly. Digging a shallow hole, I dropped the gem in and then covered it back up. I took a couple of steps back and Aki did the same. "I just needed you to bear witness to me placing the marker and its location in relation to the spring."

Aki let out a soft gasp as stone shot up six feet before curving into an arch and meeting the ground once more. In a matter of seconds, a large gateway made of dark grey stone with lines of silver weaving through it stood in front of us. "How?" Aki breathed.

"Magic," I said with a snort.

She gave me a look and then rolled her eyes. "I gathered that, but where did the stone come from?"

"The markers for gateways are crafted with a link to a pocket dimension that contains all the materials needed to construct the gateway. The daemons like to use pocket dimensions for all sorts of spells. It's kind of their thing."

"It's amazing." Aki tentatively trailed her fingers across the surface of the stone.

"It's convenient." I shrugged.

"Are there other species besides daemons who can use pocket dimensions?"

"None that I've encountered," I said. "Actually, I did meet a warrior once who could summon a sword out of thin air. His magic likely relied on a pocket dimension of some sort, but I never asked for the specifics."

Aki gave me a wry grin. "I can see why you would be more impressed with a weapon appearing out of nowhere than a bunch of stone."

"I am a fan of weaponry." I patted the dagger strapped to my thigh. "Let's head back inside. We're gonna leave as soon as the sun rises tomorrow, and I want everyone to be rested." I walked with Aki back to the cave and stopped at the opening. She turned back when she realized I wasn't following her.

"Aren't you going to come in?"

I shook my head. "I'm going to stay on watch here, just in case. I can go days without sleeping, so I'll be fine."

She studied me. "It's because we have our empathic magic back, isn't it? You're worried that we'll read your emotions."

"Yes, but probably not for the reason you think. I don't care if you read my emotions on a deeper level. I already know what you'll find. Right now, all of you trust me, that would likely change if you knew who I truly was. I don't need that complication right now."

"You really think that our opinion of you would change that easily?"

"Yes."

"I think you give us too little credit."

"Tell you what, once we make it safely out of this realm. I'll let some of you read me and we'll see who was right."

"I'll hold you to that."

Chapter Ten

At the first hint of light in the sky I went to wake the Kalari up. They'd spent most of the night talking about their newfound magic and what it meant for their kind. Then they'd started practicing, laughing as they tried to trick each other with different emotions. They loved their magic.

Part of me hated them for it.

My shifter magic was the only part of me I didn't have to hide. As soon as the rest of my magic had manifested, my ability to open gateways and absorb the magic of others, my parents had hammered one thing into me. I had to hide it. It wasn't something to be used, enjoyed, or celebrated. It was something to bury deep within myself and never speak of.

"Come on," I prodded Aki with my foot as she looked up at me with groggy eyes, blinking slowly. "Y'all got five minutes and then we're out of here."

She mumbled something in response that I couldn't begin to understand, but rose and started waking the others. I nudged a few more with my foot to get them moving and then went to wait outside. I walked a short distance from the cave mouth towards some crystal pillars and crouched next to them. My head tilted as I examined another circle of upturned dirt that definitely hadn't been there yesterday. We'd walked right by this crystal formation and I would have noticed. Unease ran through me as I scanned the surrounding area. Nothing else stood out.

"Something wrong?" Aki asked as she and the others joined me.

"Not sure. But something alive has been here recently."

Aki looked at the bit of upturned earth and frowned. "The same thing that left the trail on the mountain?"

"I'm assuming something like it. Let's get moving and keep a fast pace. If we need to stop, we can, but let's try to keep the breaks to a minimum."

"We can do that."

We set off at a brisk pace. Whatever excitement the Kalari had been feeling had been replaced with wariness. They remained silent and alert as we weaved our way through the crystal forest. When we'd made it roughly halfway back, I stopped to take a drink of water and allow the others to rest. Aki and several others were sitting on a long crystal that had fallen against several others. I tucked my water back in my bag when I felt the hairs on the back of my neck stand up. I slowly spun in a circle, taking in the surroundings, but not seeing anything. But I knew what my instincts were telling me.

Something's coming. Something's coming. *Something's here.*

I pulled my sword free. The quiet conversation the Kalari had been having died.

"Get up on the crystals," I said, keeping my voice low. "As high up as you can."

To their credit, they asked no questions and quickly helped each other climb up the large black crystal formation. I flicked my wrist a couple of times, spinning the blade as I loosened up my muscles. A surge of magic was my only warning, and I leapt to the side as the spot I'd been standing seconds before exploded and a creature surged out of the ground.

"What type of beastie are you?" I asked in a low and wicked voice as I studied it quickly, looking for any weak points to attack.

The legless serpentine-like creature swung its eyeless head towards me and opened up a mouth full of teeth that curved backwards. Dirt and ashes covered its thick brown scales. Another two shot out of the dirt, closer to where the Kalari were hiding up on the rock. Luckily, they weren't long enough to reach the kids. The biggest one was close to fifteen feet long and I was guessing its thick body weighed several hundred pounds. The one closest to me was momentarily distracted by the newcomers appearances, but then it turned its attention back on me and let out a sound that was more a screech than a growl.

The sound felt like it pierced my eardrums, but I gritted my teeth through it. The creature lunged towards me, it's long body closing the distance faster than I thought it capable. On liquid joints I slid to the side and slammed my sword through the center of its head. It flailed wildly, ripping the sword out of my hand before falling still.

The other two that had been circling the Kalari paused, scenting the blood in the air. They obviously didn't hunt by sight. The question was, did they hunt by sound or did they rely on their ability to sense magic?

"I killed your buddy!" I called out and quickly moved to retrieve my sword from the fallen devourer. "You gonna do something about it?"

No reaction.

I stretched my hand out, letting some of my magic out to open a gateway. The two creatures screeched in unison and rapidly moved in my direction. That answered that question, and it removed any doubt about whether these were devourers. I let the magic fade.

I'd never encountered devourers like these before, but I had fought against devourers that hunted in packs. Whatever these were, they weren't pack hunters. There was no coordination in their attacks and when one of them dove in, I was easily able to slide out of the way and it rammed into the other. They went down in a tangle and I took a few steps back and paused in front of a narrow midnight blue crystal that was lying on its side.

The two devourers snapped at each other as they untangled their long bodies. Sliding apart, they swung their heads back and forth, trying to detect me. I let some of my magic rise again and the one on the right let out a blood-curdling sound before barreling after me.

When it was less than five feet away, I leapt up onto the crystal and braced myself as it slammed headfirst into the solid wall. Before it could recover, I dove off and sunk my sword into its head. The long, heavy body jerked a few times before collapsing.

Two down. One to go.

The remaining devourer reared up, even with only half its body off the ground it towered above me. I ran and sliced across its side, but my blade bounced off its thick scales. Stabbing worked, but slicing was out. Faster than I thought it capable of moving, its head snapped down towards my left side. I tried to spin out of the way, but I was a fraction of a second too slow. Its jaws closed around my thigh and a scream tore out of my throat as I felt dozens of teeth dig into my flesh. Two things happened immediately. Its earth magic rose, and it sank into the ground, pulling me with it. At the same moment, its devourer magic tried to absorb my magic.

I felt the second its magic touched mine, and it reeled back as if shocked.

"That's right, asshole," I hissed, jerking myself free from its loosened grip.

The devourer recovered quickly and moved to bite me again. This was either not one of the smarter species, or it was so hungry that it was in a frenzy. Devourers couldn't absorb the magic of other devourers, the magic cancelled itself out. Of course, they could usually kill you with their teeth and fangs easily enough and they wouldn't turn down a meal of flesh and bone.

My magic was already working to heal my thigh. I limped back a few feet, keeping my weight on my other leg as much as possible. The devourer slid forward, and I slashed across its side again, knowing I wouldn't do any damage, but hoping to bait it into a strike. This time when it snapped at me, I was ready and dropped flat on my back. Its massive head slid over me. I gripped my sword with two hands and drove it up into the beast's skull. It tried to jerk its head away and I shoved the blade in deeper until the creature finally stopped moving. With a grunt, I dumped it on its side next to me.

I let go of the sword and laid there panting for a few moments. My skin itched where my magic was slowly piecing it back together.

"Are you okay?" Aki called out. "Is it safe for us to come down?"

Smart of her to ask if it was safe before just leaping down. I pushed myself up and examined my leg. Aside from being a little sore it was fine and more than capable of bearing my weight. It would be good as new within the next ten minutes. My fingers traced the pieces of my shredded pants. Those teeth were designed to hold on to their prey as they dragged it underground to devour its magic. I was lucky the thing hadn't torn my damn leg off.

"You can come down now," I called out.

While the Kalari carefully got down off the crystal formation, I pulled my sword free from the devourer's head. My nose wrinkled as I sniffed the blood and then wiped it off as best I could on the hide of the beast before sliding it back in its sheath.

"What are they?" Aki asked as she and the others carefully approached the dead beast.

"Likely the devourers that caused your ancestors to flee this realm." I prodded it with my foot. "Some type of reptile. They have earth magic. That's how they're able to burrow into the ground so fast. And how they survived while the volcanoes were erupting, they hid underground."

One of the Kalari boys crouched down next to its head. "It kind of reminds me of the glass lizards we have in the human realm. But bigger obviously." All of us looked at him blankly, and he grinned. "I used to catch them when I was younger. They're legless lizards. People always think they're snakes because they don't have legs. But if you look at them closely you can tell they're not. The shape of their heads is wrong and their movement is not the same as snakes." He shrugged. "These things are the same."

"Lizard, snake, whatever the hell these things are, I doubt these were the only three in existence. We need to get moving," I said. "They likely have been using the springs to stay alive, feeding off the magic. It's been enough to keep them alive, but only just. They came after us because all of you now have magic and it was enough for them to sense. I can keep mine mostly contained, but empathic magic is harder to hide and all of you are new to it. You're basically ringing the dinner bell for every starving devourer still alive in this realm."

They all paled at my words, but Aki looked at me curiously. "How were you able to get away from that last one? It latched onto your leg and started pulling you into the ground, but then it stopped and loosened its grip enough for you to get free."

I hated it when the clients I was working for were observant. "It tried to adjust its grip on me and I was able to pull free," I lied. "Everyone up for jogging? We still have several hours to go before we get back to the others."

"We'll manage," Aki replied, and the others nodded in agreement.

"Let's go." I took off before Aki could question me further.

Chapter Eleven

A few miles from the large flat rock we'd left the rest of the Kalari group, I felt the brush of earth magic. It was faint, but there. A second later, I felt another. Then another. *Shit.* We wouldn't make it. I wasn't sure the Kalari were even capable of flat out running at this point, although the fear and adrenaline might be enough to push them further. But even if they flat out ran, those things would be on us before we reached that rock. I needed to distract them and buy Aki and the others time.

I kept walking, but started stripping off my weapons and handing them to whoever was close to me. "Take these," I told them. The Kalari carefully took the weapons I handed them, confusion on their faces, but did as I asked without question. "The devourers have caught up to us. There are too many for me to fight and keep all of you protected. I'm going to distract them, and all of you are going to run like hell to that rock. Get on that rock and stay there, understand?"

"How are you going to distract them?" Aki asked.

I stopped and pulled off my mask, boots, and clothes, wrapping them in a bundle I handed to Aki. Several of the

Kalari kids blushed and most looked away from me. Growing up with the humans had clearly made them uncomfortable around nudity. Aki's attention never wavered as she held my gaze.

"I'm going to shift," I told her. "It'll take me a minute, but the process is going to send out a huge pulse of magic. The devourers will key in on me. As soon as I'm done shifting, I'll roar. You run. Got it?"

"Got it." Aki tucked the bundle containing my clothes and boots under one arm. "How can we help once we make it to the rock?"

"Don't worry about me." I shook my head. "Just make it to that rock. I don't think their earth magic is strong enough to get through rock that thick."

"You don't think?" the youngest of the Kalari squeaked.

I gave them a wicked grin. "We'll find out soon enough. Run fast."

Before they could panic any further, I sank to my knees and let my shifter magic out. "Start walking," I said, my voice more a growl than anything else. "Don't start running until you hear my signal."

"Come on," Aki said as she got everyone moving again. "Good luck, Nemain."

Speech was beyond me, so I trusted her to get all the Kalari walking towards the rock as my muscles, bone, and skin shifted. A minute later, I rose and shook out my coat. My bright golden fur stood out in this bleak landscape.

The air tasted even more foul in this form and soon my magic would have to start healing my lungs, but I ignored the burning feeling. As expected, the devourers had focused on me. I could feel them closing in. I threw my head back and roared. Aki and the others took off at a dead run.

I spun and ran to the side, maintaining the same distance from the rock where the Kalari were gathered. Small formations of rock and crystals were piled around, nothing as tall as the large rock that would hopefully protect the Kalari, but it would have to be enough for me to lead these devourers on a merry chase that ideally didn't end with me being torn apart.

Just as I reached the first small formation, the ground under me exploded. A snarl ripped out of me as I was flung in the air, barely managing to twist enough to land on my feet. Another devourer burst out of the ground between me and the crystals I'd been aiming for. I could feel more closing in behind me. I couldn't stay here. It was game over if they surrounded me.

The devourer that'd cut me off lunged forward with open jaws, but I was already running back the way I came. It screeched and gave chase, more of them leaping out of the ground, flinging dirt in my face. I pushed my long legs as fast as they could go and barely managed to stay ahead of them.

Some continued to chase me above ground, but the smarter ones dove back beneath the surface and used their earth magic to propel themselves forward. I could sense the bursts of their magic, but not specifically enough to know when they were going to snatch me from beneath. Another crystal formation jutted out of the ground on my left, its sharp edges beckoning me forth. I altered my course and aimed for it. Diving between the devourers as they leapt out of the earth.

One of them clipped me when I was fifty feet away, sending me spinning. I recovered just in time to jump out of the way as another dove up out of the earth and crashed into the one that had nearly grabbed me. They screamed in rage and temporarily ripped into each other, allowing me to escape.

Three more took their spot and barreled after me as I ran towards the large crystals. I allowed myself a precious half second to slow and gather myself before pushing up off the ground, leaping clear over the jagged edges. The two devourers that leapt after me fell short and impaled themselves on the crystals. They screamed and flailed, trying to get free, flinging dark purple blood everywhere.

I kept moving, aiming for the next formation in the distance. Out of the corner of my eye, I saw the Kalari kids make it to the flat rock. They helped each other toward the top, where their family could grab them and pull them up. I needed to buy them another couple minutes before I could get to safety myself. The ground trembled, and I felt the largest surge of earth magic yet. Something was coming, and it was big.

Crap. This wouldn't be good.

I wrung every last drop of speed out of my body and scrambled up onto the rock just as the world exploded behind me. I whirled to face the threat, claws digging into the rock, and froze. The new devourer dwarfed the other ones. Long bony protrusions rose from the back of its spine, with smaller ones running along its sides. As it raised its massive triangular head, I saw the soft scales of its belly. My claws and teeth wouldn't do enough damage. I glanced towards the Kalari and saw Aki being pulled up. All of them had made it to the safety of the rock. It was time for me to do the same.

The rock I was on was only six feet off the ground. It was enough to keep the smaller devourers at bay, but not this one. Its head rose until it towered above me and then it flung itself forward, massive jaws gaping open. I spun and jumped off the crystal, breaking into a run as soon as my paws hit the ground. The giant devourer roared behind me and the ground trembled as it hit the dirt once more. The smaller devourers screeched and chased after me. I ran towards the Kalari who were screaming at me to run faster. The ground in front of me trembled and another giant devourer surged out of the earth.

Shit.

With the other one behind me and the smaller ones almost flanking me, I was boxed in. I couldn't outrun them forever. One stumble and I'd be a goner. I stayed the course, heading straight towards the newcomer. Its long body stretched out, not coiling like a snake, but instead blocking as much as my way forward as possible. The devourer behind me let out another roar. It was closing in. The one in front raised its head, getting ready to strike. My heart beat wildly, and I didn't hesitate as I ran straight for it. It snapped forward, its maw opening wide to swallow me whole.

I leapt at the last possible second and landed on its head, claws digging in. It screeched and flung its head back. I used the momentum to push off and gain that much more ground. I spared a glance over my shoulder and saw the large devourer that had been closing in on me had veered off course to avoid slamming into the other one.

They could move fast in a straight line, but they weren't that agile and doing so cost it speed. The smaller ones had to alter their course as well, but they didn't slow down nearly as much. I kept running. The Kalari were all standing at the edge of the rock. Aki shouted something at them and waved. They quickly moved back, giving me space to land.

As I neared, I slowed down just enough to gather my strength and then I sprung. My body slammed into the rocky surface, my front paws scraping for purchase on the top. Rear claws digging in, I scrambled up the remaining distance and turned to make sure the devourers couldn't reach us.

Half a dozen smaller devourers circled the base of the rock, letting out strange chuffing sounds. The two larger ones followed slowly. They stretched out their heads until they bumped into the rocky walls. I felt their earth magic rise, and the rock trembled slightly, but held firm. I slumped in relief. Their earth magic wasn't strong enough to get through this much rock.

We were safe. I could take the Kalari home and be done.

But they could never return here. The daemons wouldn't build a gateway to this realm with active daemon activity, even if these particular devourers did seem fairly easy to kill. Technically, it wasn't my problem. I'd done my part of the job. It wasn't my responsibility to help them any further. I looked at Aki. Relief shone in her eyes, and I sighed. It was probably for the best that Jinx hadn't come, because I was about to make a really dumb offer.

Chapter Twelve

Aki passed me back my clothes and swords after I finished shifting. I nodded in thanks and slid every-thing back on. Another Kalari passed me my throwing daggers, and they all silently watched as I put all my blades away and double-checked the straps. I knew they were all brimming with questions, but they held them back as if they knew I needed a few minutes to collect myself.

The devourers had circled the rock a few times and then retreated once more to the earth. If I wanted to, I could reach out with my own brand of devourer magic and see if I could still sense them. But I wasn't sure how much of a handle the Kalari youth had on their new magic or what it was capable of. They couldn't see magic like the fae and a few other species could, but it seemed likely they would be able to sense it. Being so new to their magic, they might not be able to tell what exactly my magic was, but I didn't want to risk it. I very much doubted the devourers had left the area anyway. I didn't need my magic to confirm those suspicions just yet.

"This is a good news, bad news situation," I said. Sekeela and several of the other older Kalari pursed their lips. "The good news is that we found a spring, confirmed that it does indeed give the Kalari back their empathic magic, and I placed the gateway marker near its opening."

"I'm guessing those devourers that trailed all of you here are the bad news?" Sekeela asked, sadness touching her features.

"Yes." I explained my theory about how the devourers had survived all this time and why they'd honed in on the kids. "I take it you know what this means?"

"The daemons won't establish a gateway near the spring, and they will permanently close up the one they opened for us to get here," Sekeela said in defeat. The other Kalari glanced at each other in alarm and confusion.

"It's rare for the daemons or fae to allow travel to realms that have confirmed devourer activity," I explained. "You're lucky that you've even been able to get the daemons to open these temporary gateways over the years. There are many who have tried over the centuries to return to their home realms, but been unable to get the daemons or fae to open a gateway."

"So that's it?" Aki asked, her expression tight with frustration. "We've found what we were looking for, only to lose it again? We brought some water back with us from the spring, but we have no way of knowing if it will still work. And it's not nearly enough for everyone anyway." The others echoed her sentiments, but I found Sekeela watching me with those kind, warm brown eyes.

Damn it.

"There is a solution," I said. Everyone stopped talking and looked at me. "It's simple, really. Kill the devourers. Problem solved."

Silence reigned before Aki asked. "You can do that?"

"I'm good at killing things," I said matter-of-factly, a few Kalari shifted uncomfortably. "And I've gone up against far nastier devourers than these ones."

"But there are other springs in this realm, or at least there were." Aki frowned. "Aren't there likely devourers in these areas, too?"

"Most likely," I agreed. "If the goal of your people was to return to this realm, then that would be a problem. But you only need to get to the spring we found. If we can kill the devourers in this area, chances are pretty good you'll be able to work something out with the daemons."

A tentative hope spread across the Kalari. "How?" Aki asked. "How will we kill all the devourers?"

"Not 'we'," I said and tapped my fingers on my chest. "Me."

Aki arched an eyebrow at me. "You expect us to just stand by while you take on all the devourers by yourself?"

"Oh, no." I grinned at her. "I'm going to set a trap for them, and all of you would have to play a very special part in that."

"What?"

"Bait."

* * *

I waited for several hours before venturing off the rock to see if the devourers were still lying in wait. After a few circles around the rock, increasing my distance a little each time, I decided it was safe enough to put our plan into action.

First, I surveyed the area where I planned on setting the trap to make sure it would work then I went about drawing more of the devourers out by running around in my feline form all night. I made sure to choose an area where there were lots of tall rocks for me to jump on for safety. It still wasn't an experience I ever cared to repeat, but I was confident that any devourer in the area had come to investigate this new source of magic. Then I shifted back to my human form and waited for them to calm down and snuck back to the rock with the Kalari at dawn.

While I'd been away, the Kalari had been hard at work preparing for our plan. They'd packed up all their gear and made a makeshift stretcher to carry Bahir on. He'd tried to insist that he could walk, but one stern look from Sekeela had shut him up.

I'd tried to convince the older Kalari to let me send them home now, but they'd refused to leave the younger generation behind. We'd compromised on them going through the gateway first before putting the rest of the plan into action. It still meant they'd have to make the dangerous trek with the rest of us across the open plains to where I would set my trap.

"All right, everyone. Let's do this." I headed over to Bahir. The others would carry him on the stretcher, but it would be easier if I jumped down with him.

Before he could object, I bent down and scooped him up. He let out an indignant sigh, but didn't complain. Aki and Sekeela were ushering the others to jump down carefully. I took a step off the rock and tried to keep Bahir as steady as possible as we landed. Sekeela and some others were there almost immediately and helped transfer him to the stretcher. The four Kalari carrying it adjusted themselves while Sekeela checked on Bahir. Aki smirked from the front of the group.

"You're just happy that Sekeela has someone else to fuss over so she leaves you alone," I told her as I approached.

"You're not wrong."

I watched the last of the Kalari climb down off the rock. "Remember the plan everyone. Stay together, it should take us less than an hour to reach the canyon. For those of you with magic, I know you're not in full control yet, but do your best to not use it. Things are going to get real interesting if the devourers find us before we set the trap."

"I don't think 'interesting' is the right word to use," Aki said dryly.

"Would you like me to get more descriptive about what will happen?" I arched an eyebrow at her and she just grinned at me. I rolled my eyes. "Let's go."

Even though we knew the devourers didn't hunt by sound, everyone remained quiet as we made our way to the canyon. We made it in just under an hour with no signs of the devourers. I didn't want to hang around any longer and test our luck. I pulled the red gem wrapped in wire out of my satchel and faced the others. "I'm going to use this to open a gateway." I held the gem up for everyone to see. "The gateway is going to open into a forest outside a daemon run town in Mexico. It'll be a short walk into the town once we're there."

Sekeela looked at Bahir in concern. "You can't open it closer to the town? Or in the town?"

"The daemons wouldn't appreciate me opening a gateway within the town's borders." Truth and lies. They wouldn't like it because it wasn't supposed to be possible. If I opened up a gateway in the middle of a daemon town they would have all sorts of questions for me. Sekeela frowned, but before she could push any further, I continued, "As soon as I start opening the gateway, any devourers close to us will sense the magic. We'll get everyone through who needs to be, then Aki and the others will be up."

Striding over to the canyon edge, I held the gem out in front of me. My magic unfurled and pulsed from my hand causing the gem to glow from within. The Kalari behind me sucked in a breath. I made sure to keep my expression one of neutrality as the gateway started to open. The gem had been primed by the daemons to use for enchantments and other spells, it would have reacted to any magic that was active around it. But it looked impressive and that's all that mattered.

The air in front of me shimmered before tearing open and revealing a vibrant, lush rainforest. I'd been to this rural region in Mexico recently and I knew the forest was usually empty in this area and thus low risk of anyone seeing the gateway. The daemon who ran the bar in the nearby town would likely be curious about how we'd ended up there, but if I dropped Pele's name they'd quickly stop asking questions.

"Step on through." I stepped back and waved towards the gateway.

Those who were carrying Bahir went through first, slowly lowering the stretcher once they were out of the way. Sekeela waiting for everyone else to go through before pausing in front of me and Aki.

"Please be careful." She took Aki's face in her hands and kissed her forehead.

"They'll be following the rest of you in a few minutes," I told her. Sekeela nodded and then joined the others on the other side of the gateway. "All right, kids. Time to fire up that magic."

Aki's brows furrowed in concentration as she accessed her magic. The rest of the Kalari youth bore similar expressions.

I studied the barren lands in front of us, but didn't see or feel any devourers. "You need to kick your magic up a notch," I said.

"We're trying," Aki said through gritted teeth. "I think because we've already practiced on each other it's easy for our magic to do it again."

"Try me."

"Are you sure?"

"I told you I'd let everyone read me at the end of this." I met Aki's eyes. "This is the end of the ride. No concerns about lack of trust after this."

Defiance flickered across Aki's face. "I'll always trust you."

I looked away. "We'll see."

The empathic magic dug deeper, and I pushed back against it enough to force the kids to work harder for it. Their eyes took on a luminance as their magic tried to pry into my soul. I felt some of it creeping towards the magic I kept chained deep within me and I opened another part of myself. The empathic magic followed the easier path away from my hidden magic. To the scars across my soul, left by the things I'd done over the centuries that should have haunted me but didn't. They would have haunted a good person. But my chances of being a good person ended the day my parents were murdered. The blond Kalari boy who had found the cave stumbled away, his eyes fading back to their normal color as he looked at me in horror. I smiled at him, fangs fully on display. He paled and took several steps back until he was through the gateway.

"Keep pushing," Aki told the others.

More of them had taken steps away from me, but they didn't release their magic. The first brush of devourer magic hit me, followed rapidly by several more.

"They're coming. Move closer to the gateway, but don't go through yet. Keep pushing with your magic. When I tell you to, get through that gateway as fast as you can. Wait for me in the forest, I'll join you when it's done."

Aki and the rest moved towards the gateway, sweat running down their faces as they kept pushing at me with their magic. The ground started to vibrate causing ash to rise into the air, it looked almost like smoke billowing out of the earth.

As the devourers converged on us, several smaller ones leapt out of the earth. Likely to get out of the way of the bigger ones. They screeched as they slithered rapidly towards us.

"Go! Now!" I yelled.

All but Aki dropped their magic and fled. Sekeela had moved to the gateway, but remained on the other side as she beckoned for her granddaughter. The young Kalari looked at the advancing devourers and then back at me, uncertainty flashing across her features. I knew she would be reluctant to leave me behind but I needed her to get the hell out.

"Go, Aki!"

She dropped her magic and joined her grandmother on the other side.

Dozens of small devourers were above ground now. I could feel at least six large ones beneath the surface plus more small ones that hadn't been crowded out yet. The earth shook as if it was being ripped apart and I struggled to keep my balance at the edge of the canyon. The timing had to be perfect. My magic snapped out, slamming the gateway closed mere seconds before the earth exploded in front of me, raining down dirt, rocks, and ashes.

Trusting my instincts, I dove forward directly in-between two massive devourers. Their large bulky bodies twisted as they tried to change course, but they were too slow. Their momentum carried them forward, right over the edge, and they plummeted into the canyon below. Many of the smaller devourers were carried over the edge as the larger ones slammed into them. Screeches and bellows raged as they fell only to be cutoff as they were impaled on the jagged crystals lining the bottom of the canyon.

I didn't have time to celebrate how well my plan had worked. The larger devourers were taken care of along with at least half of the smaller ones. But there were still more than a few left, and they were all focused on me now. I moved before giving them a chance to attack. I struck quickly and brutally with my blades, killing three before the others realized what was happening. I ground my teeth as their screeching threatened to rupture my eardrums. Sinking my sword into one I tried to duck under another's attack only to trip over the tail of another. The air whooshed out of my lungs as my back slammed into the ground. A gaping mouth came at me from the side and I rolled to the side, straight into the jaws of another. I screamed as it bit down on my arm and drove my other sword into its skull.

Shoving its jaws open I pulled my arm free and tried to keep it tucked against my body as best I could. I was down to one good sword arm and still had several devourers left. Peachy. The remaining devourers circled me, snapping at each other when they got too close. Hmm.

I didn't second guess myself as I slid my remaining sword into its sheath and ran towards the largest of them. I leapt onto its back and ran up its spine until I was holding onto its neck. It flung around trying to get me off, striking another with its tail.

That one shrieked angrily and bit down hard onto the tail of the one I was clinging to. My grip started to slip and I shoved myself off to the side as the devourer I'd been clinging to dove at the other one that was still ripping into its tail.

They went down in a tangle of snapping jaws and thrashing tails. Swiping my other sword off the ground I whirled towards another one that hadn't been distracted by the infighting. It rose up as high as it could before diving forward aiming for my legs, I jumped straight up and brought my sword down. It's head went one way and its body the other.

I cut down another two and then looked around, panting. The two that had been fighting had managed to deal fatal wounds to each other. One was still clinging to life as its blood pooled around it. One quick strike put it out of its misery.

Just to be sure there weren't more underground, I waited a while and then started opening gateways. Not to where the Kalari were waiting for me, but to other realms that didn't have any inhabitants. I poured magic into the gateways, but no more devourers came forth. Minutes ticked by and still none came. Finally, I let all the gateways close and opened one more to take me home.

Chapter Thirteen

The Kalari had remained exactly where I'd left them in the rainforest. Sekeela and Aki looked at me in relief when I appeared, but there was a wariness that ran through most of the younger Kalari now. The ones who had used their empathic magic to dig into my soul.

I met each of their stares with an expression of indifference. All but one glanced away, the boy who had been the first to withdraw his magic and retreat through the gateway. He stared at me now with a mix of fear and disgust. Aki cleared her throat and stepped in between me and the boy before he could say anything. "Is there anything we can do for your arm?"

"No." I shook my arm out to the side. "It's already mostly healed. It just looks bad because of all the blood. Let's head to town."

The Kalari picked up Bahir's stretcher and followed me through the rainforest. Within thirty minutes we reached the small town and crossed through the ward that kept most humans out. Unlike the taverns in Tokyo and Cairo, this one was located in a town that was completely run by daemons. It was far away from any major human populated areas.

I didn't even know why the daemons had built a town here in the first place, but it was convenient for me to use when I needed a place out of the way. We made our way through the narrow streets, getting a few stares from the locals, but nobody stopped us or questioned us. Weird things happened in daemon run towns and nobody worried about it unless the daemons declared it was something to worry about.

"The tavern is this way." I turned onto the main street that ran through the town and walked towards the largest of the buildings. I swung the door open and held it as the Kalari obediently followed me inside. A daemon with red skin so dark it was almost black looked up from where they were clearing some tables. Matching black eyes latched onto mine, amusement flickering through them.

"Nice to see you again, Nemain."

"And you, Toci." I let the door swing shut as the last of the Kalari trailed in. "Would you mind helping us get to the Cairo location? I'm completing a job for Pele and we just need to get back to Cairo to wrap everything up."

"Of course. Anything for a friend of Pele," they said slyly as their dark eyes roamed over my torn clothing and still healing injuries looking for any clues as to what trouble I'd gotten myself into this time.

Toci was relatively young to be in charge of a tavern like this, only two hundred years old. Most daemons that age were still traveling around the realms having fun, but Toci was ambitious. I'd have to keep that in mind and either limit my traveling through this town or make sure to come here under less suspicious circumstances.

"Just give me a few moments to get everything ready. Feel free to rest at the tables."

"Thank you."

Toci nodded and disappeared into the room next to the bar.

I settled down at one of the tables and looked my arm over. It was still sore, but all the wounds had closed up. Even with the recent fights with the devourers, my healing ability was back in full force. That should be enough to satisfy Pele and get the lead she promised me. Then I could go and collect Jinx and we would be on our way. Movement caught my attention and pulled me out of my planning as Aki sat down across from me.

"We made it," she said quietly.

"We did. Soon you'll be back in Cairo. You'll have to discuss any future plans with the daemons, but I'll confirm that all devourers have been wiped out in that area. That should satisfy them to activate the gateway close to the spring. Then the Kalari can decide if they want to have their magic back or go on living as they have been."

Aki nodded, but didn't say anything. Her expression was troubled as she stared at the table between us.

"I told you." Her eyes snapped up and met my stare. "Knowing who I am. What I'm capable of. It changes things."

"It does," she said evenly.

A small pain flared in my chest, but I smothered it. I knew this would be the outcome. I focused my attention on the door that Toci had passed through, wanting this to just be over.

A hand fell on my arm, and I looked back at Aki. "You were wrong though. I still trust you, Nemain." She rose and went over to help Sekeela who was arguing with Bahir about whether or not he could stand up.

I stared at the dried blood on my arm, unsure how to process what Aki had said.

Before I could dwell on it much further, the office door swung open and Toci announced the gateway was ready. I got up and walked over to where Sekeela was still arguing with Bahir and swiped him off the stretcher. "It's in the job description that I'm responsible for each of you making it back to Cairo safely. Wouldn't want you to injure yourself further between here and the gateway." I winked at him as he glared at me with fake outrage.

I carried him across the room and carefully maneuvered through the doorway. Nodding at Toci I continued through the gateway into the Cairo office where Sura greeted me. As the rest of the Kalari came through, I gently set Bahir on his feet and made sure he was steady before letting him go. He groaned slightly as he stood tall, but he remained standing. "You should have a daemon healer look at you, they should be able to finish healing any broken bones."

"But then Sekeela will stop fussing over me." A bright smile spread across his face and I couldn't help but smile back at him.

* * *

The only sound on the beach was the tide rolling in and out. I breathed in the salty air as I leaned back on my elbows. After all the Kalari had arrived in Cairo, Sekeela and Aki had filled in Sura on everything that had happened. I spoke up a few times to clarify some things, but otherwise remained quiet.

Sura said it was likely the daemons would be willing to open up the gateway near the spring much to the relief of everyone. I'd gotten cleaned up in one of the rooms upstairs and Sura had provided some clothes for me to change into. She'd also offered to open the gateway back to Tokyo, but I'd needed some time to myself.

Sekeela had cried as she thanked me for everything that I'd done. Between her tears and Aki saying that she still trusted me after seeing so much of who I truly was...I wasn't ready to go back to Tokyo. Instead, I'd asked Sura to send me somewhere I could find a quiet beach. She hadn't asked any questions, only said that she knew just the place.

It was night time now and I had the beach all to myself, not that this particular beach was ever crowded. The fae ward surrounding this area ensured that few humans would ever reach this section of the beach and the fae rarely came to the human realm. I stared at the blue flower tattoos that wound about my arms. My birthday was only a few hours away, which meant another one would be burning itself into my flesh soon. Most of the time I ran on pure hate and rage, it's what got me through every day since Myrna's death. But never on my birthday. Today I just felt tired.

By now Jinx, Pele, and Kaysea would likely know I was done with the job and was back in the human realm. Jinx was almost always by my side and Pele and Kaysea usually made sure one of them was with me on this day. They'd be worried and looking for me, but I'd needed this time to myself. The tide was rolling in and it gently ran across my toes.

"I miss you, Myrna," I whispered. "I never deserved you. And you died because of me. I'll never forgive myself for that."

I sat there until the water was almost up to my waist then I stood up to return to the tavern. It was several miles down the beach and I could use that time to collect myself before turning to my friends.

The sound of footsteps drew me up short and I whirled around, swords drawn in one smooth motion. My blood ran hot and cold at the same time when I saw who had joined me on the moonlit beach.

"Greetings, my love. I've missed you," Sebastian said, a satisfied smile spreading across his face. "I was worried you wouldn't make it back in time for your birthday."

"I'm going to kill you." I took a step forward, but then forced myself to stop.

Sebastian was a lot of things, but he wasn't reckless. This was a trap. It had to be. The grip on my blades tightened as I scanned the area, keeping one eye on the warlock. Something was very wrong, but I couldn't figure out what.

"I think I can change your mind, but we should move our conversation somewhere else. I feel like we have some bad history with beaches."

A cottage on a beach flashed in my mind. A light, musical laugh. Warmth. Love. Blood.

A growl tore out my chest as I moved towards Sebastian. Trap or not, I would cut out his heart. Just as I raised my sword, a whip cracked and wound around my wrist pulling me off balance. A second one followed, wrapping around my other wrist. I strained against them, but they held firm.

In a blink, someone was behind me and kicked the back of my legs and I crashed to my knees. I screamed in rage, and in that instant, I realized what I was missing before. My magic wasn't there. It should have been tearing at the chains to get free, but there was nothing. I reached for my other magic and tried to open a gateway, and pain tore through me instead. I gasped and leaned forward as much as I could, panting against the pain.

Sebastian strode towards me, tossing a small pouch up and down in one hand. "Ah. I see you've finally noticed this fun little creation of mine. I won't bore you with the details, but suffice it to say, while you're in the vicinity of these pouches, none of your magic will work." I shook my head trying to focus on his words, but it was so hard to concentrate.

"What...what did you do...to me?" My words slurred. Sebastian crouched in front of me and held out the pouch. I blinked trying to focus on it.

"This little one packs a bit of an extra punch and dulls your senses. Couldn't risk that feline sense of smell detecting my vampire friends before we were ready, now could I?"

At his words several vampires joined his side, including the two who held the whips that still bound my wrists. I hadn't even realized that I'd dropped my swords. I gulped in air, trying to clear my mind, but the world was spinning around me. *Jinx?* I thought frantically. *Help. Please help.*

But I was too far away. He wouldn't hear me and none of my friends knew where I was. There was no help coming. I would simply disappear and they wouldn't know where I'd gone. Blackness encroached on my vision increasing my panic. I fell onto the sand, my eyes closing.

"It's time for you and I to have a long overdue chat. It's time for you to come back to me."

Sebastian's words drifted through my mind and then there was nothing, but darkness.

Nemain's story continues in A Shift in Shadows. Read the first two chapters now!

A Shift in Shadows Excerpt
Prologue

Darkness was never something I feared. Quite the opposite, actually. It was something I sought out for comfort. To feel safe. When I was young, I believed I was the creature to be feared by everything that went bump in the night.

I thought myself invincible.

Almost four centuries of living taught me just how wrong I was. But even after I realized there were things even I had to dread, I still harbored no fear of darkness itself.

Until *they* took me.

And shattered my soul.

The room that currently served as my prison was so devoid of light that even with my exceptional night vision, I saw nothing. No shapes. No outlines. No hints of anything. No windows and no clocks, making time infinite.

That was one of the many ways they tortured me. And there *were* many.

"Ah, good. You're awake," a pleasant voice said in the darkness.

A snap sounded, and soft light filled the room. I blinked

rapidly, trying to adjust my vision. Clear, light blue eyes met mine.

The warlock waited until I was focused on him. "How are you doing this beautiful evening, my love?"

"Fu-fu-fu—" Spasms ran through my cracked and dry throat before I could force the rest of my words out.

The vampires working for the warlock had already visited me for their nightly entertainment. One of their favorite games was to see how much pain I could handle before screams finally tore out of me. I'd choked down my cries as they shattered each finger bone. But I broke when they began crushing the bones in my legs.

My magic had healed the more serious injuries first, leaving my throat sore. Under normal circumstances, I would have healed myself within minutes, but my magic was running a bit low these days. The warlock sitting across from me made sure of that. In addition to the vampires essentially using me as a juice box, he had crafted a potion that made it hard for me to think and weakened my magic, all except for healing. He only wanted to break me, not kill me.

Sebastian always was a clever one.

When we'd been lovers, he'd used that cleverness to charm and entertain me. That had been so long ago; it was hard to remember a time when I had loved him instead of hating him with every piece of my broken soul.

It's amazing how much can change in a century. Now Sebastian uses his spells to torture me in an attempt to bend me to his will.

I was fairly certain my stubbornness would outlast his cleverness, but my mind wasn't exactly firing at all cylinders these days, so that might be wishful thinking.

Sebastian clucked his tongue and moved towards me. I tried to shift away, but they'd tied me too tightly to the metal table I currently laid on. Panic rose as I pulled against the ropes. Memories of being bound and powerless in my youth flooded my mind.

I reached for my magic even though I knew I would find nothing but emptiness. Sebastian gave me a small smile.

Gods, I hated that smile.

"I'm so sorry it had to play out like this," he murmured. His eyes looked me over sadly, and I wanted nothing more than to claw them out. "I would have preferred to keep things between us a private affair. You would have come back to me eventually, I'm sure of it. But things are changing, and my hands are tied."

He lifted a hand and stroked my cheek, fingers trailing down my jawline and brushing against my lips. I held perfectly still, biding my time.

"The others don't know you're here. They think I'm still looking for you. But I can't hide you forever. And they will do far worse to you once they have you." His thumb brushed gently over my bottom lip once more. "Agree to work with me, and this will all be over. I can protect you from them. You loved and trusted me once. We can put the past behind us and be as we once were. Together. Unstoppable."

I snapped my teeth. He yanked his hand back with a glower, but not before I drew some blood. My tongue flicked over my lips, and I savored the sweet, coppery taste.

"I will never come back to you." I sank every scrap of strength left in me into those words, my voice coming out strong and even.

Rage flashed across his features before the smooth, charming façade settled back into place. "I'll see you soon."

He snapped his fingers, and the lights went out.

I closed my eyes, not that it really mattered, and listened. Sebastian was gone, and my body relaxed as much as it could while bound this table. I had no idea when he'd be back. Some-

times he'd be gone for long stretches of time. He never partici-
pated with the vampires in their torturous games. But he was
the one in charge, so he was responsible all the same. Sebastian
had always preferred psychological torture over physical.

My ears picked up on a slight shuffling sound outside my
door. The guards were probably bored. I don't know why they
bothered; no one had come for me, and it seemed unlikely
anyone would do so now.

I wasn't sure exactly how much time had passed, but Sebastian and his vampire cronies had kidnapped me on my last birthday. And he hadn't mentioned my birthday again. There was no
way he wouldn't have brought it up and made some sort of
perverse celebration around it. So, less than a year. My friends
and family likely thought I was dead.

If only. Death would be a gift.

My heart ached every time I thought about them. They'd
been so worried about me and my never-ending quest for
revenge against Sebastian. They'd pleaded for me to stop, at
least for a while, instead of continuing to throw my life away as I
tried and failed to kill Sebastian for decades.

It was all for nothing. I had failed, and he had finally won.

All I could do now was continue to deny him until he finally
lost his patience and killed me. Or until the vampires went too
far and drained me dry in their games. I hoped Sebastian would
at least leave my body somewhere to be found by my loved ones,
but he was a vindictive enough asshole to deny them that.

I had started to drift off when I heard one of the guards gasp,
followed by several thuds.

My eyes shot open. Bodies hitting the floor?

Two of the thuds sounded lighter than the others. I craned
my neck to look in the direction of the door, even though I
couldn't see anything. A few seconds later, the door swung
open, and light filtered in from the hallway.

The scent of a cool rainy night drifted into the room, and I went completely still.

Impossible. There was no way he was here.

I had finally gone insane, and my memories were fucking with me. Or I had drifted off to sleep and Sebastian was using his ability to weave dreams to mess with me.

Despite my disbelief, I couldn't stop myself from inhaling that familiar scent. It'd been centuries since I'd smelled it, but I would never forget it.

"My apologies for taking so long, child," Magos whispered quietly while cutting me loose from the steel table.

I said nothing as I studied him quickly and efficiently cut me loose. Last I'd seen him, his hair had been long and contained in tight braids. Now it was shaved close to his scalp. Other than that, he appeared the same as he had the day I'd saved his life by being a nosy child with very little self-preservation instincts.

"Are you real?" I whispered as he helped me stand.

His copper eyes burned bright with anger, making them stand out even more against his dark brown skin. "Yes, I'm real. I'm sorry I didn't come sooner. Your family and friends have been looking for you. When I heard you were missing, I did my own investigating. Some old contacts claimed a shifter had been captured by a group of vampires aided by a warlock. I took a chance on it being you."

Maybe I'd finally lost it and was hallucinating this conversation. I rolled my shoulders back and shifted my weight, savoring the ability to move. It *felt* real.

Hesitantly, I reached out and touched his arm, trailing my fingers down towards his hand. He held a sword with a slight curve. Mist still clung to it.

The tentative hope I'd been feeling settled deep within my chest at the sight of the blade.

This was real. It had to be.

"I take it you can't shift or use magic?" His voice was gentle as he looked me up and down, but his face hardened the longer he looked at me. The torn-up tank top and underwear I wore left most of my flesh on display. There was no hiding the bite marks, cuts, and burns all in various stages of healing.

"No." I shook my head vehemently before stopping and forcing myself to focus on his question. "No magic. No shifting. They dose me with a potion every morning to block that." I licked my dry lips. "It clouds my thoughts, too."

"I'll get us out." With slow but urgent movements, he led me to the door and out into the hallway.

Pain flooded my still-healing body with each step, and I latched onto that to help push back the fog that settled over my mind. We stepped over the headless bodies of the guards and continued down the dimly lit hallway.

The vamps hadn't bothered to keep the house in any decent shape. The wood floor was worn, some lights were missing bulbs, and the '70s-style wallpaper was peeling or completely missing in some areas. Random statues and paintings decorated the hallway. They'd likely killed or turned the owners ages ago and used this as a feeding house. My nose wrinkled at the stench of rot leaking from some of the other rooms. Furious shouts came from somewhere deep within the house.

"Stay behind me. And stay close." Magos ran out the door and down the hallway.

I followed, trying to push away the questions bouncing around in my head. *How much time has passed? Why had he come by himself and not gone to my friends and family if they were looking for me? Are they okay?*

"Escape first. Ask questions later," I mumbled. I didn't have a clue where the exit was, but my intuition was adamant I should trust him.

Even if he *was* a vampire.

"Come on, Nemain! Move!" he called out in that melodious accent I'd never been able to place.

We soon reached the end of the hallway and turned around the corner, and my vampire rescuer shoved me to the side. I slammed into the wall. Magos was fast, but not fast enough. I bit back a scream as the blade that had been aimed at my heart buried itself in my shoulder instead. Pain erupted as it tore through flesh and bounced off bone, ripping free with more damage.

A growl rumbled out from my chest. They'd been slicing my flesh without any fear of retaliation for so long that they'd forgotten who I was. What I was capable of. It was time to remind them just who they'd been fucking with.

I ducked when the dagger-wielding vampire struck at my chest. A familiar heat spread through my muscles as I rotated until my back was against his chest. Grasping his hand, I pulled it back until his wrist snapped and he dropped the long dagger. I snatched it out of the air and slammed an elbow into his face. The vampire's head snapped back, blood pouring from his nose. My arm flew in a move based on nothing but muscle memory and sliced through his throat. He gurgled as his hands clenched at his neck, trying to hold back the blood gushing out between his fingers.

My fist slammed into his face once more, and he collapsed to the floor. With one downward motion, I shoved the blade through his mangled neck. I rose as his head rolled away from his body.

I tried to focus on where Magos was and the rest of the vampires, but it was so hard to think. The fog that was ever-present in my mind thanks to Sebastian's potion had lifted slightly during the fight, but now it was pressing back in. I gripped the blade harder and willed myself to stay here in this moment.

A loud crash from behind made me jump, and the lights went out. My back was against the wall, but all I could hear was my frantically pounding heart.

Panic rose as I struggled to stay calm, breathing becoming difficult as my lungs refused to expand. The fog's pressure intensified, and my thoughts kept slipping away, replaced by doubts.

Maybe I'd been wrong. Maybe this was a trap. A new method of torture to break me.

I could still smell Magos, but too many other scents were present for me to pinpoint his precise location. My chest tightened further as I gripped the blade like it was the only thing keeping me anchored to this reality.

The sounds of bodies crashing into each other and snarls came from farther down the hall.

If this was real, I needed to get my shit together and help Magos, but I couldn't convince my feet to move from where I was rooted against the wall. Someone grabbed my arm, and my body moved on pure instinct.

I broke his hold and threw a punch but missed. I froze and listened, trying to pinpoint his location. *Got it.*

I spun and kicked out with my right leg. He danced out of reach, and I couldn't tell where he was. I shook my head, but whatever was in that potion made my head fuzzy. *Focus, damnit.*

Before I could throw another punch, my attacker grabbed me again but just as quickly released me.

My fist flew forward in his general direction only to be caught in someone else's much bigger hand. I hissed as I tried to pull free until moonlight filtered in through the nearby window, as if a cloud had hazed by, allowing a glimpse into the night sky.

I relaxed when I saw Magos in front of me, holding a very dead vampire in his other hand.

"It's rude to assault the person rescuing you. I've taken care of the remaining vampires, but I'm sure more are on the way. Also, you should watch your language." His face was turned away from me, but I was pretty sure he was grinning.

"You could have said something," I muttered.

Although, given the bodies on the ground, it looked like he'd been busy taking out several more vampires while I'd been having a minor panic attack. I looked down and saw another vampire at my feet. Well, his headless body anyway.

Magos disappeared around the corner, and I ran after him, down the stairs and out the front door. A break in the clouds allowed the full moon to light up the sky.

I slowed, breathing in the crisp night air. I was free. *Free.* But then the adrenaline coursing through my body faded and shock settled in. Before I could process much more, Magos pulled on my arm, and we took off at a sprint once more.

He glanced over his shoulder at me. "I have a car on the other side of the gate at the end of the driveway. We just have to make it there, and then you can rest."

I jerked my head in a quick nod and pushed my body to run a little faster as we fled into the night.

A Shift in Shadows Excerpt
Chapter 1

I woke with a start, gasping for air as my vision narrowed. Tears tracked down my face, and I frantically reached behind me, my fingers slipping under the pillow and curling around the handle of a dagger.

Breathing in, I focused on the feel of the cool, rough handle. My fingers traced the slight dip where a piece was missing.

My dagger. My bed. My room.

Slowly, the panic faded. I was free. No ties held me down. I let out a long breath, released the knife, and rolled onto my back. Sebastian may no longer have me, and he may have failed in binding me to him, but he had succeeded in breaking me.

I'd never been much of a crier, but now most mornings I woke up with puffy eyes and dried tears on my lashes.

Not that I'd been the picture of good mental health before I'd been captured. But that me, the one who ran purely on rage and the need for vengeance, felt like a distant memory. She was still there, lurking beneath the surface, usually making an appearance when something caused me to lose my temper.

But now there was this other layer between the new me and the old me. One filled with tears, panic, and numbness.

I hated it, but I didn't know how to fix it. And while I also hated the panic attacks, a small part of me enjoyed feeling numb after being so angry my entire life.

The magic inside me, however, felt... differently.

It despised the numbness.

Every time I had a panic attack, it would surge forward and try to break free. Sometimes I was able to shove it back down, while other times it succeeded, and we had to go into damage control mode to get it contained again. Clean up whatever mess was made. I'd destroyed more than one home since Magos had rescued me.

Outside the large windows that took up an entire wall of my bedroom, the sky was starting to lighten with the hint of sunrise.

I sighed. Whatever nightmare I'd been having must have been a doozy, but at least my magic remained safely contained. And *he* hadn't come to visit me in my dreams.

Any time I went to sleep and didn't have to see Sebastian's face was a gift.

I was still tired, but I knew there was no going back to sleep at this point. A quick glance at the digital clock next to my bed told me it was 5 a.m. I had been asleep for a whopping two hours. Ugh.

After rolling out of bed, I walked over to my dresser and pulled on a pair of stretchy black pants and a dark grey tank top. The large bedroom was sparsely furnished, containing only the bed and a modern dresser with two matching night-stands. The only personal effect I had rested on the dresser, a housewarming present from my best friend, Kaysea. A large electric blue flower rose from a thick stem that had smaller vines wrapped around it. A few long green leaves stretched outward.

Once the sun came up, they'd twist toward the window to soak up the rays. The flower picked up on my movement, turning its deep orange center towards me. The thick petals surrounding it trembled as it swayed back and forth slowly.

It must be hungry. I frowned. When was the last time I'd fed it? Two days ago? Maybe last week?

"I'll feed you soon," I promised.

The vines started to unwind, and I quickly left the room before they finished. It wasn't dangerous, but it was grumpy when hungry, and I didn't feel like getting slapped in the face. As soon as I stepped foot in the hallway, I heard the coffee grinder start up in the kitchen. Vampire or not, my roommate was simply the best.

A small part of me expected to wake up and find Magos gone one day. I had saved his life once, so he had saved mine. But the debt was repaid, and he didn't owe me anything else. Plus, he was a vampire, and I wasn't exactly on good terms with vampires these days.

But he had stayed by my side this whole time. Nursed me back to health and helped me as best he could when my magic raged out of control.

I'd tried to push him away in the beginning. I wasn't a safe person to be around. But nothing I did could make him leave, and finally I gave up trying. Now I didn't know what I would do without him. He was my anchor in the chaotic storm that was my life.

When I'd reached out to Kaysea and my other best friend, Pele, after getting free, they'd both been so relieved to hear from me. Kaysea had cried tears of joy, and Pele had cussed me out for being stupid enough to get caught in the first place. But once Pele was done throwing a bitch fit, she'd offered me a place to stay. I'd refused at first, both because I wasn't one to accept charity and because my control over my magic was too volatile after I'd first gotten free.

But Pele had eventually convinced me to come by

promising to arrange gigs for me to take once I was feeling up for it in exchange for rent.

My magic had been tamed enough that I'd accepted under one condition: Magos came too.

She hadn't been thrilled about that part. Vampires weren't well-liked in the magical community, and after learning vampires had worked with Sebastian to capture me, my friend's dislike of vampires only increased. That she'd conceded to my request and allowed Magos to stay in the apartment and even gone so far as to adjust the wards for him spoke to just how worried she was about me.

I was glad I'd taken Pele up on her offer to move here. Before Sebastian had captured me, I'd been planning on visiting Pele in Emerald Bay. While she lived in the daemon realm, she ran the tavern of the daemon-run town on the Washington coast. I'd grown up in the human realm, and it was easier for me to travel around here. Whenever I was in the fae and daemon realms, I had to worry constantly about anyone looking too closely at my magic. But in the human realm, all I had to do was slap on a glamour and I was good to go.

It didn't hurt that I loved the old mill that Pele had renovated into three apartments. She claimed she'd done so with the intention of using it for visiting friends and family, but this one had been furnished to my tastes and overlooked the rocky coastline.

She'd even gotten me a motorcycle to ride and claimed that it "came with the apartment." I had no doubt she'd done all this when she'd learned I was alive and free. She'd wanted me to have a safe place to stay.

Pele was never one to talk about her feelings, particularly mushy feelings, but she always showed them with her actions.

I walked up to the bar in the kitchen and slumped onto one

of the stools. My hand flopped out onto the countertop, and my fingers made a "gimme" motion.

Magos's eyebrows rose slightly, but he handed me a mug. I took a sip. Perfect.

"Did you work as a barista at some point in your life? Is that how you've been occupying yourself these last few centuries? Seems like that'd be difficult with the whole vampire thing. Or did you manage to find a coffee shop open only at night?" I tilted my head and arched an eyebrow at him.

Magos seldom smiled, but the corners of his mouth twitched as he strolled out of the kitchen.

I sighed and settled in to enjoy my coffee. Despite living together for almost a year, I barely knew anything about him. Figuring out his past had become a bit of a game between us, one I was sorely losing.

With his dark rich brown skin, short-cropped hair, and strange copper-colored eyes, Magos was jaw-droppingly gorgeous. At just over six feet with broad shoulders and a strong chest, he drew attention any time we left the house.

He pretended not to notice, but I was always entertained by all the stares he received from women and men. Granted, humans were pulled towards vampires regardless of their looks to a certain degree, and the older the vampire, the stronger the pull. Magos claimed they couldn't help it. I remained unconvinced.

Regardless of his ridiculously good looks, there had never been the inkling of anything romantic between us, despite what my brother and some of my friends believed.

Magos and I had met when I was a child. To be fair, that meeting had been fairly brief—less than a day, in fact. But when you save someone's life, you tend to remember it. I wasn't sure how to define our relationship now. I'd never had much in the way of family, only my parents and brother. But I supposed Magos would have fit well into the role of uncle.

I enjoyed my coffee and stared out the window, trying to ignore the unease that was always lurking in the back of my mind.

My friends and family had worked so hard to make me feel safe here, and I felt guilty about not being okay. Part of me wanted to run. Disappear somewhere in the human realm or one of the other realms for a while. It's what I usually did when things in my life went to hell.

But after centuries of running... I was tired. So instead, I shoved the feeling away and watched the waves crash into the rocky shoreline.

Pele truly had found and designed the perfect home for me. Similar to my bedroom, the rest of the apartment was sparsely furnished. The main living area was one big space that consisted of the kitchen, living room, and a workout area. The living room held a couch and a few chairs that faced a large TV. The rest of the space was dedicated to sparring and weapons storage.

"Up for some sparring?" I moved towards the large sparring mat without waiting for Magos's response.

No art hung on the bare brick walls. Only weapons. Lots and lots of weapons.

They had been the first thing I'd started to collect when we'd settled down here. My main swords hung next to the front door, but my collection of throwing knives and just-in-case-shit-really-hits-the-fan swords hung on the brick wall behind the sparring mat.

I walked past all the blades to grab my favorite fighting staff and twirled it in my right hand.

Besides being a clean roommate who served as my personal barista, Magos was also my sparring buddy. Shapeshifter healing is remarkable. It'd taken me only a few days to fully recover after escaping the vampires. Physically, at least. We'd started sparring shortly after that. I'd been training with my swords since I could hold them as a child. And after my parents' deaths, I threw myself into training even more. It was rare to encounter anyone with the skills to go up against me in a one-on-one fight.

Magos kicked my ass every time. It didn't matter what we chose—short swords, longswords, staffs, freaking nunchucks—the end result was always the same.

I usually grumbled a bunch of swear words in as many languages as I knew while Magos helped me back to my feet. I hadn't beaten him yet, but over the past couple of months, I'd made him work a lot harder to get me down.

Magos nodded, walked across the mat, and grabbed his favorite pair of bastons. The two-foot wooden sticks didn't look intimidating, but I was well aware of how much they hurt when he landed a hit with them.

He made no comment about me being up again so soon after going to bed. He had probably heard me screaming. Nor did he comment on me wanting to spar again after he'd given me quite the beating earlier in the night. He knew both the coffee and the sparring helped me settle.

Neither of us were good at talking about our past, but we *were* good at helping each other in other ways.

"Just going to stand there? Afraid I'll mar that beautiful face of yours?" I crooned.

As usual, he didn't move. Just stood there with a calm, easy expression in the middle of the mat as I circled around him.

"My apologies. I thought you wanted to exercise your body, not your mouth. You can assault me verbally just as well if I'm seated, can you not?" he said dryly.

Before my clever retort could come out, he spun around and

slammed one of his bastons into my staff. I pushed back, only to receive a blow to my ribs with the other one. I bit back a cry and jumped out of his range.

We continued to circle each other, looking for openings.

"Plans for the day?" He closed the distance between us.

I blocked the blow to my right side and spun out of range of the follow-up coming to my left. Not quick enough. I felt the sting on my shoulder as I backed away.

"Going to check in with Kaysea this morning. She was planning on meditating to see if she could trigger a vision. If she's foreseen anything, I'd like to know. Might check in with Pele, as well. And I need to convince Andrei to spend my birthday here." My tone stayed steady even though the mention of my birthday quickened my pulse.

I moved to the left and stabbed with my staff, but he easily blocked it. I spun behind him and gave two more quick thrusts. Also blocked. I danced out of reach before Magos launched a counter offensive. He studied me calmly as I moved around him.

"There are no signs Sebastian knows where we are. It's unlikely anything will happen on your birthday."

"I know." I feinted towards Magos's left. He didn't fall for it. I made a face at him, and he just rolled his eyes. A habit he had definitely picked up from living with me. "I just don't want to be caught unprepared. He might not know where we are, but we also don't know why he worked with those vampires to kidnap me. He's been content for decades to torment me all by himself. Something must have changed.

"Since we don't know what, I want to err on the side of caution. Kaysea will be safe in the fae realm. Pele, likewise, will be safe if she remains in her bar. Andrei is the obvious target and the weak link. He'll be safer here with us."

"Very well."

Then he *moved*. One moment we were circling around each other and the next I was blocking his blows as fast as I could. My staff shook each time it blocked a blow, and despite pushing myself as fast as I could, I had only a few more seconds before his blows made it past my defense.

Just *once*, I would like to get him on the mat. Winning was out of the question. Unless I used my magic, which I never did when we sparred. Magic wasn't something that could always be counted on. I'd learned my lesson on that.

Magos's technique was perfect. Every move was as graceful as it was deadly. He spent just enough energy for each strike and nothing more. Magos fought with perfect control, whereas I fought like a wildcat who had just escaped from its cage... which wasn't exactly far off.

I lunged towards him and jabbed with my staff. He knocked it aside, and I let it go as he swept me off my feet as I'd anticipated.

But I didn't land on my back like he expected. Instead, I arched my spine and reached out with my hands; as soon as they hit the ground, I pushed myself back and landed on my feet in a crouched position. Feline shapeshifter agility for the win! Launching myself forward, I pulled an absolutely stupid move that only worked in the movies. I crashed into Magos's knees, and we both ended up on the mat.

I reached for my staff, but before I could move, he switched our positions and was straddling me and pushing the wood baston against my throat. Game over.

Laughter erupted from his throat as he looked at me with amusement dancing in his eyes. He smiled so rarely, let alone laughed so freely. I might have lost the match, but I still considered this outcome a win of sorts.

"Satisfied? Can I return to my chair and coffee now?" he asked, still smiling.

"Sure. I'm going to lie here for another minute and enjoy my moment." I might not have beaten him, but I still got his ass on the ground.

Of course, I'd lost the match. Lost. Just like I'd lost the fight when the vampires had jumped me years ago.

My smile slowly faded.

I closed my eyes as the panic I'd fought back less than an hour ago rose again. My chest tightened, making breathing difficult, but I forced myself to maintain steady breaths. Something told me today was not going to be fun.

Want to Read More?

The next book in the series, A Shift in Shadows is out now! Signed paperbacks with character artwork are available on the Greymalkin Press Shop at www.greymalkinpress.com.

Author's Note

Thank you so much for reading *A Shift in Darkness*! I got the idea for this story while I was working on the second book in the Lost Legacies series, *A Shift in Fate*. Because I was on a deadline for that book, I had to put my idea on the back burner for a bit.

But as soon as I sent the manuscript for *A Shift in Fate* off for editing, I immediately started writing this novella. It was a little challenging to write because I didn't have all the characters from the previous books to draw from since this story takes place before A Shift in Shadows. On top of that, I didn't want to repeat information from other books either. But despite these challenges, the story came together really well, and it was so much fun to write!

If you enjoyed reading this book, it would be incredibly appreciated if you could leave an honest review on Goodreads, Amazon, or whichever platform you prefer. Reviews are incredibly important for authors and we really appreciate it when y'all take the time to leave one!

Curious about how Nemain and Kaysea met? Want to read other short stories set within the Lost Legacies world? Sign-up for the newsletter at maddoxgreyauthor.com to get free short stories and stay informed of upcoming releases and events!

And lastly, if you're on Instagram or Facebook, feel free to follow me there! I'm most active on Instagram these days and regularly post what I'm reading, random bookish content, and snippets from my current work-in-progress.

It would be wonderful to keep in touch with y'all!

About the Author

After earning a degree in history and political science, Maddox was pulled kicking and screaming from the world of academia and thrust into the tech industry. Because they had bills to pay and nerd muscles to flex.

Whenever possible, they leave reality behind to build fantasy worlds filled with snarky morally grey characters and hot but devious love interests. Maddox currently resides in the northeast, but they'll always consider themselves Californian at heart. They live with their partner and faithful, but often stinky, furry companions.

To get regular email updates about new releases and other announcements, be sure to sign up for the newsletter on maddoxgreyauthor.com

facebook.com/maddoxgrey.author

instagram.com/maddoxgrey.author

tiktok.com/@greymalkinpress